E. Lynn Linton

Grasp Your Nettle

Vol. II

E. Lynn Linton

Grasp Your Nettle
Vol. II

ISBN/EAN: 9783337044091

Printed in Europe, USA, Canada, Australia, Japan

Cover: Foto ©Andreas Hilbeck / pixelio.de

More available books at **www.hansebooks.com**

GRASP YOUR NETTLE.

A NOVEL

By E. LYNN LINTON,

AUTHOR OF THE "LAKE COUNTRY," ETC.

IN THREE VOLUMES.

VOL. II.

" Tender-handed stroke a nettle,
 And it stings you for your pains;
Grasp it like a man of mettle,
 And it soft as silk remains."—AARON HILL.

LONDON:

SMITH, ELDER AND CO., 65, CORNHILL.

1865.

GRASP YOUR NETTLE.

CHAPTER I.

In a small apartment in the Rue Saint Antoine sat a dark-haired, pretty little woman of about thirty-five years of age; but so beautifully dressed and so cleverly made up, that she did not look more than twenty-five at most—unless you took her in a cross light, and then you could see the blanc de perle and the rouge de Vénus lying in the tracings by which time had begun to tell the world that Madame Louise Trébuchet was passing to the shady side of her youth.

She was a small woman, and it was a small

apartment; what we should consider almost a doll's-house; in which a well-developed Saxon, or a six-foot Hibernian could not have stood or turned. It was à l'entresol, where you could touch the painted ceiling with your hand; and consisted of but three "pieces," a kitchen, a living-room, and a dressing-closet without a window; the whole three capable of being put into a well-sized packing-case and bundled off by a sturdy porter to Sainte Pélagie, Madame Louise Trébuchet included.

But if minute, it was perfect; as dainty a little apartment as could be found in Paris. The chimney-glass in its bright gilt frame, with rosettes of painted porcelain in all the bends, which were many; the porcelain and ormolu clock, style Louis Quinze, on the chimney shelf draped with crimson velvet; the shepherds after Marmontel piping to the shepherdesses after Watteau; the artificial flowers under their tall thin shades; the bronzes; the trinkets from the Palais Royal and the " Passages ;" the marqueterie table with convulsive legs; the divan covered with crimson velvet; the étagère, all gilt and mirror and crimson velvet, loaded with Louis Quinze trifles; the easy chairs; the round pieces of carpet on the polished floor; the foot-stools; the jardinière full of flowers, but some of them artificial; and the mahogany bed in the alcove, with its crimson velvet couvre-pied, laced pillows, and white muslin curtains tied up in rosettes of rose-coloured satin—all made up the trimmest and neatest and most perfectly arranged apartment of a certain style, and belonging to a certain class of female life, to be found from the Champs Elysées to Vincennes.

It was an apartment which could hold only one person; two would have knocked their heads together; nor was there accommodation for even a servant; so Madame Trébuchet had a femme de journée for half the day, and when two o'clock came was independent and alone.

She had a great many chance visitors; generally gentlemen well dressed; and she had her " day," chiefly frequented by ladies without children, with an abundance of paint on their faces, strongly scented, and gorgeously got up in fashionable

attire and brilliant colours : a little too glaring
perhaps for perfect French taste. She was a widow
she said, without "parents" either on her
husband's side or her own, save one brother
now in England but who was often with her
when he was in Paris; and who was evidently her
brother because of the likeness. And she had
"rentes" curiously irregular in their payment;
for sometimes she was in great force, spending
money profusely on dinners, dress, and trinkets,
and sometimes she was supperless, because her
last available "brimborion" had gone to the
Mont de Piété, and she had eaten up the proceeds.
She was often compelled to live on her shepherds
and shepherdesses, and more than once had had
to turn her Louis Quinze timepiece into dinners,
if she would not have died of starvation, and soupe
à l'oiselle.

She lived a very regular and orderly life in
certain things—always in by ten o'clock, unless she
had been to the theatre or opera; and was evidently
a person of some importance to the State, for every
now and then a sergent de ville, or a commissaire

de police, would call and see her; which might have looked compromising had they not been always so wonderfully civil that the concierge thought they were her friends, or perhaps that she was a paid police agent—one of Fouché's " souricières ; " what we should translate bluntly—a spy. And this last supposition gained Madame Louise a great deal of respect.

She was an unconquerable chatterer; in speech and manner inconsequent and sieve-like ; but she had sharp brown eyes—brown shot with red— which a little belied her apparent simplicity and thoughtlessness; and for all her sieve-like talk and girlish confidences you never got so much as the shadow of any thought, fact, or circum- stance which Madame Louise did not wish you to know. She was an Englishwoman by birth and parentage, but she had been brought up in France, and was thoroughly French both in mode of thought and manner of life ; still the fact of her English birth often came in as an excuse for any solecism which it was advantageous to her to commit, and she took care to make the most of her double country. She was a charming little woman, generally dressed in black silk, with a cashmere shawl and ravishing caps and bonnets; she was good-tempered, bright, clever, supple, perfectly well-bred and not ill-educated; truly a fascinating little woman, and an acquisition to any society; but for all that she was inscribed on the police books of Paris as Louise Field, dite Trébuchet, Voleuse.

At this moment the monetary seesaw was down among the thorns and nettles; and Madame Louise sat in her pretty doll's-house considering what she could next spare, and where the gap would show least. The clock had gone; the vases had gone; the shepherd in a plum-coloured suit, flowered waistcoat, and gold-spotted pearl-grey knee-breeches, no longer piped to the shepherdess in a maize sacque and Swiss hat; the étagère was empty, and there was not a silver spoon in the place, for Madame Louise was "down on her luck," as her brother had been a few months ago. Indeed, it was partly on his account that things were now so bad with her; for since a certain fiasco that he had made, mistaking the name of one Monsieur Delaperrière, banker, for his own, the sergents de ville and the commissaires de police who "wanted" him, had been wonderfully frequent in their visits to her, thinking that they might thus get some information casually dropped which would give them a clue to his whereabouts. For Gregory had doubled on himself so closely that even the French police were at fault, and, while he was comfortably organizing his life at Clive Vale, exercised their energy and intelligence in looking for him through all the great towns of France. Even the French police may sometimes be sent astray.

But these frequent visits at home, and the embarrassing assiduities abroad of which she was the object, necessitated a ruinous caution on the part of Madame Louise, and an afflicting respect for her neighbours' goods, if she would not be pounced upon and borne off to the dreary cells she had visited once too often. And grim had been the quiet satisfaction with which they had watched this gradual eating up of her possessions, knowing

that when the last came she would trip as of
necessity, and trip straight into the arms of the law
opened ready to receive her. Madame Louise
knew this too, and was staving off the evil day as
long as she could, hoping for some safe chance to
arise which should replenish her purse, and yet
keep her free from prison bolts and bars; till now,
having parted with all her less important matters,
she must come to her " mobilier," and begin on her
chairs and tables.   It was a bitter trial to the little
woman; and her balancing between the Louis
Quinze table with the convulsive legs, or the divan
in crimson Utrecht velvet, had something almost
tragic in its equalized despair.

Time passed however, and the decision must
be made. She had had no dinner yesterday, and
she had had no breakfast to-day; all her friends
were out of town and she dared not attempt
strangers; there was not a crust of bread in the
cupboard; not an ounce of charcoal in the fourneau,
and nothing to cook even if there had been; the
last drop of wine had been drunk, and the last
spoonful of soupe; but she was still charming in

her well-fitting black silk, and her coquettish cap
of pink ribbon and black velvet would have made
many a countess envious. Madame Louise Trébuchet was wise in her generation, and never by
any chance neglected appearances, or suffered herself to be in such attire as would put her vanity to
the blush and subject her to the ignominy of being
"caught." Even when hungry she was perfect;
and she was hungry now.

Something must be done. It was past two
o'clock, and she would grow faint if she had not
sustenance, and that speedily. Something must be
done; but what? She was afraid of the old game,
for the police were watching her more closely
than ever, knowing that the cord was tightening
hourly: and yet it went to her heart to sell those
treasured bits of wood and velvet, those pledges of
her respectability undeniable to landlords. However, and she sighed, it must be; and perhaps the
seesaw would go up again soon, and lift her from
the thorns and nettles into the vineyards and the
cornfields once more. With a heavy heart, but even
though alone smoothing her face into its usual

brisk amiability, she began to dress herself for a
sortie to the well-known Mount of Piety, when her
bell was rung, and, on opening the door, the concierge delivered her a letter, "from monsieur her
brother in England" she supposed, pointing to
the English stamp and postmark.

It was fortunate for her that there was a stamp
to point to, else that too would have gone down in
the "petit mémoire" lying on the desk downstairs,
whence sometimes the locataires used to be presented with such wonderful mémoires, so imagina-
tive in their details, and so independent of
recognized arithmetic as to the summing up.

"Merci, madame!" said Madame Louise, with
her gracious ways and sharp eyes. "Yes, it is
from my brother; the first time I have heard from
him since his departure."

To which replied the porteress, "that fine-
looking gentlemen when they went abroad sometimes forgot the claims of those left at home. But
what to do? we must have patience and charity
with all people, but chiefly with fine-looking
gentlemen when out on their pleasures abroad."

And when she had concluded her little speech, she said "bon jour, madame," and trotted downstairs again; having seen with her own eyes what the femme de journée had told her some time since, that "cette gentille p'tite Ma'ame Trébuchet was on a bad road, and forced to eat up her furniture."

Madame Trébuchet's face brightened into natural sunshine as soon as she was alone; for, on opening Gregory's letter, the first thing she saw was a bank post-bill, authorizing her to receive twenty pounds sterling of real good honest gold, and no chance of a sergent de ville tapping her on the shoulder with a gruff "en avant," and tearful restitution of the same. Madame Louise Trébuchet was no Catholic, neither was she a Protestant, for the matter of that; but when the bank post-bill fell into her lap, she took out a small medal of the Holy Virgin which she wore round her neck, and kissed it repeating the Ave. She was always religious when she was in trouble, and used to pray diligently for better luck to her favourite saints, going to mass with wonderful regularity;

but not to confession. It would have been better
for her perhaps if she had. If she thought that it
would have pleased the saints, and made her more
clever in her escroquerie she would; for her religion
was only a kind of Numbo-Jumbo fetichism, and
whether Catholic or Protestant—and she was both,
or either, as occasion served—meant simply
flattering heaven into befriending her and blinding
the eyes of her victims and the detectives.

Her brother's letter was worthy of him. He
told her that he was in luck, having fallen into
a good thing which he should probably ask her
to come and share in working; but for the present
he was best alone. As a proof that he did not
forget his pauvre petite sœur, whom he was
afraid had been perhaps a little génée lately—
for he knew how his late misfortune would
sharpen certain eyes against her—he sent her
five hundred francs, which he hoped would make
her comfortable for a few weeks at all events.
He would send her more in time, and as he
could spare it. She might be sure that he
would not forget her, and he would always do

his best to make her life independent and happy. The letter was full of affectionate expressions, and many inquiries after certain of their mutual acquaintances ; and it was signed in the old way—"Gregory," no more—neither did it bear an address, or give his dear little sister Louise the faintest idea as to where the writer was or what he was doing. It was posted in London, and the whole of it was froth except the bank post-bill, and that was pudding.

"Le vaurien !" cried Madame Louise, tossing the letter on to the table ; "he is making his thousands, I am sure of it, and he puts me off with this nothing at all just to keep me in good humour till he wants me, and then I shall be the , cat and he will get the chestnuts. Why does he not tell me where he is, le chenapan ! and let me share in his successes ? By his folly and clumsiness my life has been made joliment triste of late ; he owes it to me to enliven it a little."

Which was perhaps a natural reaction against her first moment of excessive pleasure, when she began to reflect that in all likelihood this

was only a miserable per-centage, and that she
was being fed with pence while he was swallow-
ing pounds.   Still, such as it was it came in
usefully enough, as housekeepers say ; and before
the night fell Madame Trébuchet had got back
all her small penates ; had made herself up again
in gloves and boots ; had bought a " gracieuse "
little bonnet ; and had " dined," for the first
time for some weeks now, with a female friend
at Véfour's.   So she was happy and her sun was
blazing ; and though the police kept their eyes
upon her very wide open indeed, and wondered
among themselves where the money had come
from, yet they could not touch her nor despoil
her, nor mar her pleasure by fear of the evil day
to come when she would be detected and brought
to grief and shame.

It was a new sensation to Madame Louise
Trébuchet to have money honestly and innocently
got, and she enjoyed it as a youth enjoys his
first personal earnings — the " arrhes " of his
future manhood—almost sighing when she went
to bed that night, as she said to herself :

" I wish that my papa had not been such a bad man, and that he had put us into a better way of life, and then those maudits sergents de ville would have had no power over me."

It was characteristic of the little woman that her wishes and regrets went no farther than the police, and that a thought of God never troubled her small quick brain. Not that she was an esprit fort, as has been said; she prayed to the saints and the Holy Virgin vigorously for les bonnes chances in her bad career, but solely as a gambler turns his chair for luck, or as an African makes mouths at his greegre for rain or buffaloes; as far removed from the sweet trust and holy love of the Catholic on the one hand, as from the robuster and more masculine faith of the Protestant on the other. Her religion was simple superstition; but if you had asked Madame Louise herself or the concierge either, they would both have told you that she was " dévote et très bonne Catholique." If frequenting crowded churches pretty regularly, and abusing Protestantism whenever she had the chance, makes a

dévote and a good Catholic, Madame Louise was
safe, for she did both; and the last without
stint.

A few days after her brother's remittance, a
gentleman called on Madame Louise. He was
a handsome, middle-aged man, fairly portly without being fat, a little pompous in manner,
not unbefitting the prosperous father of a family,
with grizzled hair cut close to his head, and a
prodigious mass of blacker beard and whisker.
He was well dressed, and wore a big gold chain,
a big gold pin, and a big gold ring, and he gave
one the impression of great size, though he was
not much above the middle height. Still, for a
Frenchman he was tall and of imposing presence,
and carried the air of prosperity and the good
things of life—second déjeûners and diners at
les Trois Frères (all in the way of business, be
it understood) — into quite moral proportions.
He bowed courteously as he entered, and when
Madame Louise asked him to give himself the
trouble of sitting down, he took the largest of
the two easy chairs in the doll's-house, and sank

into it with the air of a man used to easy chairs
of larger dimensions.

Who he was Madame Louise had not the
remotest idea. She saw only that he was a
man of substance, and of standing eminently
respectable ; but what he wanted here, unless
he was the chef de police himself in mufti, she
did not know. However, she bore herself very
convenablement, and took out her finest airs
and graces, as she would have taken out her
best collars and cuffs, for the benefit of her
visitor and the swifter enchanting of his soul.
She talked with all her natural and assumed
sprightliness, till she talked the respectable
father of a family into boyish fits of laughter ;
and he rubbed his hands, and then his head,
in almost irrepressible mirth. There was not
a conversable subject on which she did not
touch—the opera ; the theatre—Ravel and Gil
Perez she even imitated in her pretty, childish,
bird-like manner ; le Sire de Framboisy she
hummed ; (Lambert had not then arisen ;) the
clay monkies ; and the terrible infliction of the

étrennes—(Madame Louise spoke as if half her
fortune went in these étrennes: she gave the
concierge five francs, and generally received
about five hundred); all that Paris life has of
froth floating on the surface for the moment,
she took up and touched with infinite vivacity and
agreeableness, until "Monsieur Un Tel" (he
had not given his name) thought to himself he
had never seen a more delightful little woman;
and was it absolutely true, all that was said of her?

When she had run on for a considerable time
—the gentleman watching her intently, so far
indeed as he could watch her; but the room
was dark, and she sat with her back to the light
—he then caught the ball on his side, and
began upon the darker scenes of Paris, the chif-
fonniers, the gueux, the enfants de Paris, the
lorettes, working round gradually and with really
quite artistic power to the gamblers and escrocs.
Whereupon Madame Louise, still with the vivacious smile upon her rosy lips, began to feel a
little nervous and uncomfortable, and to wonder
where he was drifting. When suddenly he said—

" Where is your brother now, madame ? We have lost him from our circle for some time."

" I do not know, monsieur," replied Madame Louise sweetly. " He has gone to Sweden—that terrible country!" shuddering : " I always think it full of wolves and bears—and will not be back till winter and the jour de l'an "—laughing—" are passed."

" Sweden ?" said the gentleman a little incredulously. " You are sure you do not mean England, madame ? "

" Oh, no ! " she said ; " he has written to me from Copenhagen."

The gentleman smiled. He was better up in his " chief towns " than Madame Louise.

" Madame perhaps means Christianstadt ? " he said politely ; and madame accepted the bridge made for her, gracefully.

" I would give you a thousand francs now on the instant, if you would tell me where he is," the gentleman said confidentially. " You would make a friend of me, my dear, for life. Come ; I know your difficulties and your exigen-

cies ; and if you would put me on the track of
your brother, for whom I have a charming little
scheme, you should not want a friend so long as
I lived."

" I am deeply grateful to monsieur," replied
the little woman casting down her eyes; "and
would willingly give him my poor brother's address, as I would willingly cast him in the way
of something good, but I am unable—I do not
know—in faith, I do not ! "

" Yet you have heard from him ? "

" Truly yes," said Madame Louise.

" And Christianstadt and Copenhagen are
neither of them so large that he cannot be found
in them,". continued the gentleman smiling, and
bending down to look into her face.

" No," said the little lady smiling too; " but
London is."

" Petite friponne ! " he exclaimed, playfully
tapping her cheek; " and so thou wouldst deceive
me, ah ! "

" Ah ! monsieur is too fine, too clever for me,"
she laughed.

And her compliment so delighted the middle-aged father of a family, who had been un peu gaillard in his youth, that he forgave her deception, and tutoied her for the remainder of his stay.

If Madame Louise could have given him her brother's address in return for a thousand francs she would, without hesitation; and she would have said, when justice had laid its iron hands upon him, that she had done it in all good faith, believing monsieur's assurances that he meant to do Mr. Gregory a service. And some among them would have believed her, because of the perfection of her acting. But she could not gain her thousand francs by any such piece of treachery; her brother was too cautious for that. So the handsome, well-appointed, well-found gentleman went away empty-handed, promising to call again soon and see how she was going on.

When he had fairly gone, Madame Louise opened the pocket-book she had abstracted from him, but found therein only some unimportant memoranda, and a card with the name of Monsieur Delaperrière, Banquier, engraved thereon.

" The old fox ! " she said, and laughed. But while she looked at the card, she wondered who would be most solid and reliable, brother Gregory or the banker? However, she sent back the pocket-book anonymously, with only one word inside — " oubliée : " and M. Delaperrière was grateful to her for her discretion.

CHAPTER II.

If Jasper, resting on the sandy foundation of a rogue's honour, had believed that Mr. Dysart would quit Clive Vale and leave him, at least for a time in peace, he was soon undeceived; for Mr. Gregory seemed making himself up for a lengthened residence, as if determined to enjoy himself to the utmost while his good fortune lasted. And whatever despair and disgust the unhappy Master of Croft might feel, the Vale was charmed when it knew that "Mr. Dysart had taken Lea Cottage, where the Lawsons lived;" and taken it for a year—Mr. Lawson wishing to remain for that time at the sea-side for the health of one of his younger children, pronounced ricketty. The thing answered perfectly for both; and the one

thought himself amply paid by the two hundred
pounds which the other agreed to give, content to
assign so much of Jasper's income for a status in
the place and the social influence resulting. So
now he was established as a resident, and took
the honours of his new condition.

Save Mr. Trelawney when he first came, and
while he was still in a manner mythic, no one
had excited so much interest in the Vale for years
as Mr. Dysart. But the interest which even
Mr. Trelawney had awakened had been infinitely
more tepid in temperature, if more solid in quality,
than that which now shed universal rose-water and
sunshine abroad. With him it had been the possible establishment of one of the young ladies, or
middle-aged unattached, and the increased energy
and vitality hoped to be infused into the graver
social life of the place—the school, the book-club,
district visiting, the missionary area, the magis-
trates' bench, and the board of guardians. With
Mr. Dysart it was his own pleasant personal attrac-
tions, the impetus he gave to the gaieties of the
Vale, and the general atmosphere of light-hearted-

ness and pleasure that he diffused, like a social Apollo as he was.

Every one felt his influence, either directly or indirectly ; and even on ladies so far removed from the centre of levity as were Mrs. Escott and Mrs. Price, he exerted his magnetic forces, and changed the current of their lives as entirely as with the youngest and prettiest of the girls. For under colour of " chaperonage," or " hospitality," or " the value of their social protection," or " the absolute necessity there was of some one of standing and irreproachable condition to take up the question and prevent its becoming vulgarised or degraded," he was pretty sure to get their help and countenance in all that he proposed ; and he balanced his pleadings with such wonderful accuracy that he secured both and offended neither. And as Mrs. Escott and Mrs. Price had always been in a manner rivals, while dear friends, in the Vale, it required no small amount of nice manipulation to drive curricle with these two for the pair ; an emergency however to which Mr. Gregory Dysart, who had manipulated more delicate matters

in his time, was equal. So that they also were
stirred out of their density and Calvinism respec-
tively, and given something pleasanter to do than
talking silly slander or sour. Which surely was a
benefit however brought about—one among the
many instances, always to be quoted, of how
strangely often the root of good lies in evil.

The Vale owed everything new and pleasant to
Mr. Dysart. It was Mr. Dysart who instituted
the archery society; and " Mr. Dysart's prize"—a
bracelet from the Palais Royal—was the first for
which the fair Toxophilites contended. (He always
called them the "fair Toxophilites," which en-
riched the Vale vocabulary by one word the more,
if it did no other good.) He established croquet
too, and tried Aunt Sally; but the Vale shook its
head at the old lady and turned her out of doors
with a sniff, pronouncing her vulgar and unlady-
like. He set the fashion of horse exercise, and
persuaded both Mr. Grainger and Mr. Campbell
to buy each a serviceable hack; or rather he persuaded them to allow him to do so—a service he
performed quite to his own satisfaction, whatever

it might be to theirs; for he got enough out of the transaction by way of secret commission money, to half pay for his own bay mare, by far the best looking animal of the three, but of too fiery a temper for any one but himself to ride, and perhaps Dr. Hale, who, as became his profession, was cunning in horseflesh.

All of which innovations caused the Vale to open its eyes as it had not opened them since Miss Aura married. And when it saw Mr. Dysart, and Miss Ellen Campbell in her hat and habit, come cantering down the village together—Mr. Grainger labouring painfully in the rear, on a long-legged brute with a Roman nose and one white stocking, said to be three parts blood by Mr. Dysart and the dealer, but which Tattersall men would have called " rather weedy"—the question was settled, the Vale thought, and Miss Ellen was held to be the future Mrs. Dysart without a chance of failure. Poor Harry Grant!

Then he got up a miniature regatta on the "lake;" an amusement of which he said the Empress was particularly fond; and he painted his own boat after the model of hers (at least so he said) and called it Eugénie. His regatta was only of toy boats set afloat with all sails set and the ladies' colours flying at the mastheads; with a prize for the winner—the one that should first drift into "Dysart Bay," as he called the little indentation where he established the station, and run up the Union Jack as the sign; and bets of "Jouvin's best" to stimulate the feelings as the sport went on. He bet in harder change with Mr. Grainger and Dr. Hale (Mr. Bennet and Major Morgan stood aloof from all this demoralization, and Harry Grant did so too, for reasons of his own both vague and definite); and as he always made more than he lost to the ladies, he could afford Jouvin's best and yet not be a cigar or a glass of grog the poorer. He looked on his prizes and gloves and all his little lady-expenses as so much popularity-seed, or as a kind of income-tax which must be paid liberally if he would retain his place in society. And after all, he was living on Jasper's money; and whenever he chose to utter a few words if things went wrong, Jasper must set him square, whatever it cost.

And beside these games and sports he gave parties and picnics without end; every week there was something afoot; and though it was only the same people again and again, still it was a more pleasant manner of passing the time than formerly, and the young people at the least were grateful and adoring. Perhaps poor old Mr. Campbell found his home less agreeable now that the girls were always out somewhere, than he used when they were more indoors, and ever ready, one or other of them, to walk with him, or play cribbage, for a penny the rubber, or backgammon for a half-penny the game, or any other of the home amusements which had hitherto been so pleasant to him and sufficing to them. And one or two others might have felt something of the same; but they kept their thoughts to themselves, and let the new reign of pleasure under Mr. Dysart's sovereignty go on unchecked. For when once a swing is given to a country place by a person who is popular, and looked up to as superior in any social acquirement, it sweeps every one away with it, and whirls down all opposition.

It was in vain that Mr. Bennet and his faithful
coadjutor the major—who, to do him justice had
never thoroughly adopted the new comer, being
himself emphatically a gentleman, if bilious and
disagreeable—it was in vain that these two stood
to their colours. They stood as in an enemy's
camp alone, and even their own special spiritual
vivandière, Mrs. Price, deserted them and carried
over white flags to the enemy. And of all
the people in the Vale, she might have been
counted on for stability with most appearance
of certainty. But she too had failed; and Zillah
and Sara were Toxophilites, and croquet players,
and picnic goers, and toy-boat regattaists, like
any of the unconverted; rivalling even the Miss
Campbells in the keenness with which they
entered into Mr. Dysart's plans, though carrying
into them less good-humoured enjoyment, and
always on the scent for "something shocking" in
secret.

"One must relax for the young a little at
times," said Mrs. Price to Mr. Bennet, when he
called to remonstrate with her against this new

clothing of his lambs in wolf-skin, and to express his dissatisfaction "at the excessive dissipation which had invaded their former quiet and Christian circle."

"One may relax, Mrs. Price, till the bow of godliness becomes a broken reed," said Mr. Bennet grimly.

"Now really, Mr. Bennet, that is being a little severe! What harm is there in anything they do? Shooting with bows and arrows is nowhere forbidden in the Scriptures that I am aware of, and if you will show me the passage I will not allow my daughters to visit the field again."

"But these pernicious bets that I hear of, Mrs. Price, what are they but gambling? and what is gambling but one of the deadly sins?"

"Oh, Mr. Bennet!" pleaded the widow a little stiffly. "I think you are making more account of trifles than need be! What are these terrible bets?—a pair or two of gloves which Mr. Dysart always contrives to lose, and which is his manner of making harmless little presents to the girls, as an acknowledgment of the hospitality that he has received from us. Do you think that I would sanction anything of serious tendency, or suffer my children to become gamblers? If he singled out one or two even, to make a distinction of, I would be the first to see the possible harm in that; but when he loses to all alike, and with so much evident pleasure in giving pleasure, I do think we may strain a point too far and make evil where none exists."

"I know, Mrs. Price, that you are a lady of high and Christian principles," said Mr. Bennet; "but I know also that we all need occasional reminders of the great truths set before us, and that the strongest of us may fail."

"I know that too, Mr. Bennet; but a Christian mother's watchfulness over her daughters may be allowed to rank with that of a pastor's over his flock, and to be as sensitive and quick-sighted towards evil," said Mrs. Price with a cold look.

And Mr. Bennet saw that it would not be well to any longer apply his clerical ferule to the grim knuckles, which, so far from receiving his blows patiently, showed a decided disposition to double themselves up and give back hit for hit.

To tell the truth, Mrs. Price was a little tired of Mr. Bennet; but chiefly tired of waiting for him for Zillah. And without acknowledging to herself that she had balanced matrimonial chances with a dash of worldliness, against Bennetism and celibacy, she yet had deflected more decidedly in proportion as she had become more and more assured that to be the curate's pet lamb and most energetic district visitor, was by no means a certain prelude to being his lawful wife. If he had been as wise as he was fond of power, Mr. Bennet would have known that his only chance now at the Hollies lay in the hope he could insinuate as a Benedict expectant, not in the castigation he could inflict as a pastor.

When the curate left the Hollies after this unusual interview with "the Dorcas," "the Deborah," "the Mother-in-Israel of his flock," as he often called Mrs. Price, it would have been hard for even Mr. Dysart—used to nice calculations—to determine which of the three disturbers of his peace he hated most—Mr. Trelawney, Mr. Dysart, or Mr. Grainger.

His equanimity was not restored by meeting the whole archery party streaming home from the ground; in the midst of whom walked the good-hearted Rector, giving his arm to Myssie Campbell with whom he had an enduring flirtation, such as innocent old rectors not unfrequently indulge in with maiden ladies young enough to be their daughters, and regarded with nothing stronger than parental feeling travestied to represent gallantry. And next to the Rector was Miss Zillah Price—decked out in the tight-fitting jacket and bandit hat with its panache of green feathers which formed the costume de rigueur of the society, while wearing also the other ungodly insignia of finger-stalls and arm-pad, the belt, the quiver, and the bow—talking and laughing with Mr. Dysart who divided her from Ellen Campbell. Sara was flirting with Mr. Grainger, who under the influence of his new friend was somewhat less staid in manner toward the young ladies than in the days heretofore, and flirted with them less in the queer stiff-backed "Old Grainger" fashion to which the sternest prude under heaven could not have objected, than in the light manner of a pseudo-rake not indisposed to a dash of pepper in his soup. What Kate and Lotty and the Rowleys were doing did not concern Mr. Bennet; indeed he scarcely saw them; wrath concentrating itself like love.

When Zillah and Sara saw their former idol come moodily along the road, looking so good and lonely and ill-tempered, they felt dreadfully naughty, and not a little ashamed; also a little frightened, which would have been more than a little had they not been supported by the presence of the Rector. But imagine the falling off there had been to make Mr. Escott's sanction any matter of comfort to them against Mr. Bennet's opposition! We show where we stand as much by our chosen champions as by our antagonists.

"Morning, Mr. Bennet," said the Rector; "you should have been with us just now, and seen Miss Zillah and Miss Ellen shoot off a tie for the gold; that's the correct manner of speaking, is it not, young ladies? It was really splendid practice, and beats the volunteers all to nothing."

"I was employed in visiting the poor and the sick, Mr. Escott," said Mr. Bennet coldly.

"Very good, sir; you could not have been better employed," answered the obdurate old Rector tranquilly. He understood the reproof of course.

"I was in your district to-day, Miss Price," continued Mr. Bennet, turning to that young lady; "and I was grieved to find that Mrs. Younghusband has been two days without a tract, and that you have suffered three to accumulate at Betsy Bailey's; also that you failed to mark down Sarah Bailey in your class-book as absent from school last Sunday, and that you have even credited her with good marks for collect, scripture, and attention, when she was staying four miles off with her aunt at Leasham. It is not often that I have occasion to point out such instances of negligence to Miss Price," he added slowly.

"I am very sorry, I am sure," stammered

Miss Zillah, blushing crimson; "but the time has slipped away so fast this week, and there seemed to be so much to get through, I don't know how it happened."

"Yes, the time has passed away very agreeably I make no doubt," retorted Mr. Bennet; "whether profitably to your own souls, or even safely, is another question. For myself I think the time spent in God's service to be better employed than that spent in the service of pleasure; which goes perilously near to sin and Satan. But then I am unfortunately in the minority at Clive Vale."

"Come! come! Mr. Bennet, I must not have my young ladies rebuked like this," said the Rector, never sorry for an opportunity of taking Mr. Bennet down. "They are very good girls, and take a world of trouble off your hands; and if they like to come out every now and then to have a little recreation, they have earned it."

"Our lives were given us for other purposes beside recreation, Mr. Escott," said the curate austerely.

"So I suppose, sir," replied the Rector a little

tartly; " but one of those purposes is not standing in the road under a blinding sunshine, listening to your sermons."

"I find my sermons are daily more and more necessary," said the curate flushing up; " the truth shall not be left without one faithful witness while I am in existence, however much others, my elders and nominal superiors, may fail."

" Very well, Mr. Bennet, bear your own witness," said Mr. Escott; " but do not make quite such a parade about it, nor bear it through a six-foot trumpet; do not kill the spirit for the sake of the letter, which is what you very puritanical gentlemen are rather too apt to do. I wish you good morning, sir, and a little more humility, Mr. Bennet—a little more humility—and less proneness to think that every one who differs from you is irredeemably corrupt, and yourself the only righteous man left in Zoar; which is too much your way, sir—and not a good way either ! "

Saying which the Rector bustled off with his companions, and poor Mr. Bennet was again left alone; the party as they went bursting into one

of those provoking fits of laughter which seem to
express derision of the one just left, and which
are always so interpreted; though in general they
are caused by something quite foreign and un-
connected. As to-day; the outburst that came
from all, so soon as they had left the curate,
being due to a pun which Mr. Dysart flashed
round the circle to make them laugh, so that
Mr. Bennet might think they were laughing at
him.

"There, Miss Zillah, you have got yourself
into a fine mess with your master!" said the
Rector, as they swept along the road in their fine
array, walking all across it five abreast. He liked
to have his little joke with the two Misses Price
about their young master as he called Mr. Bennet,
and to let them see in a good-humoured kind of
way what two simpletons he thought them.

"Mr. Bennet is very good, but he is very
strict," said Miss Zillah in a tone of apology;
"and we can only take people as we find them—
their bad qualities with their good."

"Humph!" said Mr. Escott, "that is not the

usual creed of Clive Vale, I think; eh, Miss Campbell?"

"No, I wish it was!" laughed that young person in her cheery, rather metallic voice. "If we had more charity we should have less scandal amongst us, and I am sure Clive Vale is the most scandalous place in England!"

"Oh, but we must draw a line!" said Zillah. "And though I said that we must take people as we find them, with all that is admirable in them and sometimes with what is not quite so good, that does not mean that we are to consent to sin or to look lightly on evil."

"A wise and liberal distinction I think, Rector?" said Mr. Dysart approvingly.

And Zillah Price was proud, and almost forgot that Mr. Bennet was offended.

It seemed though, as if the archery meeting to-day was destined to disturb many hearts; for still on the way home, and very shortly after Mr. Bennet had been disposed of, they came upon Harry Grant walking quickly along the road as if he had been coming from Croft; as indeed was the case, with Mr. Trelawney's "instructions to sell" in his pocket. Harry, too, hated the archery meetings and all the rest of the new gaieties, as people generally do who cannot join in them; but he hated them chiefly because they were of Mr. Dysart's prompting. And Mr. Dysart he both feared and doubted.

Just as he came up his enemy was saying something in an under tone to Ellen Campbell, which made her laugh and blush. She did not want the new grace of emotion to make her more seductive to poor Harry; for indeed she looked quite pretty enough as it was; her green jacket and steeple-crowned hat with the coquettish plume setting off her pretty figure and piquant face to full advantage.

It was nothing very treasonable, though, that Mr. Dysart was saying; it was only, "Does Miss Ellen Campbell know the fable of Diana and Endymion, with its present application? Or is it the story of Iphigenia and Cymon that she is now enacting?" glancing at Harry.

But Ellen rather vehemently declared that she

did not understand Mr. Dysart at all, and could not make out what he alluded to or meant; and, as her corollary, was so decidedly cool to Harry whom she would have been ashamed to have favoured for fear of Mr. Dysart's jests, that the poor lad went away broken-hearted, and would have given all his fortune to have been able to take Mr. Dysart by his coat collar and kick him out of the Vale.

As Gregory went up the village after having seen the Miss Campbells home, he met little Hannah Marks with a small basket on her arm—it was the memorable flower basket which he had carried that day of the High Cross Bridge meeting—but it was filled with tracts, not flowers, to-day; for though by no means a pet lamb, she had not deserted the post of duty as Zillah and Sara had done, but was off now to her "district" as patiently and meekly as if there were no pleasures in Clive Vale in which she would like to join, but could not. She was but twenty; and in all her quiet primness there was young blood if cooled, and a girl's natural desires however strictly held in check.

For the first time in her life Hannah had of late wished that "aunty" was rich, and felt half disposed to envy the more fortunate young ladies, whom hitherto she had only admired and liked to see happy, without a thought of equality or of herself. But now she wished that aunty was rich, and that she had a green jacket and a bandit hat with feathers like Miss Ellen Campbell and the rest of them, and that she might "shoot off ties for the gold," and get the prize which Mr. Dysart both gave and presented. Now, for the first time too, she quarrelled with herself, and took exception to the soft flaxen hair and light blue eyes which hitherto she had neither noticed nor cared about, and which in reality made her greatest charm; wishing that she was tall and strong, with crisp black hair and sparkling black eyes— in fact like one of the Miss Campbells, who were decidedly Mr. Dysart's favourites; Miss Ellen being supreme. It was a new sensation to Hannah to notice herself at all; the kind of "finding out" that most young girls come to some time in their youth, and that forms the first great epoch in their mental lives when they do. And it was a disagreeable one; weighing her down with a sense of personal unloveliness as well as of social insignificance, which, added to her natural timidity and shyness, made her days one long hour of shame and self-dissatisfaction.

But, wishing or not, her place was not among the aristocrats of the Vale. She was petted not adopted; which made all the difference; and though Mr. Dysart would willingly have made a stand for her if he had dared, yet he knew "it would not do," and that in so censorious a place as this a too open patronage of the little maid would be damaging to him—and to her too. Not that he cared for that, if he had got his own account by it. But it would do him no good to have his name coupled with hers, he thought; nor did he care to have it known that he had made a conquest of her; while any supposition of playing with her would have done him irreparable mischief. So the poor child, unprotected by any one, was left out of all the extra gaieties lately inaugurated. She had no archery costume; no

toy boat; no croquet sticks or hoops; no pretty
riding-habit with the jaunty collar and manly tie
and hat and gauntlet gloves belonging; but she
went to the picnics and the tea parties, and she
always joined in the long walks which, under the
name of "botanical rambles," were great occasions
to all concerned.   Aunt Dess was well pleased that
she should join in those for the " good to be had
from Mr. Dysart's large botanical information ; "
and by this time too, Hannah herself believed
that Mr. Dysart understood the subject indepen-
dently, and not only just so far as he was told by
others.

"Ah! Miss 'Annah ! " cried Gregory as they
met, while Hannah's fair young face flushed as he
spoke ; " out on some good errand as usual?
Why do you not join the archery society, hey ?
You would make a first-rate shot after a little
practice."

" Aunty cannot afford it," said Hannah
simply.

" Diantre ! and I suppose she would rave if
I were to present you with the accoutrements

and costume?" said Mr. Gregory in an under voice.

"Oh! that would be impossible, if you please, Mr. Dysart," said Hannah.

"It would do you good, it is capital exercise," returned Mr. Dysart. "Cannot you persuade aunt Dess, as you call her, to let you join?"

"I wish she could," said Hannah wistfully; "but I know that she cannot afford it, and I would rather say nothing about it to her. She does not like to refuse me anything, and it would be selfish in me to ask her for what she cannot give."

"Then why do you not get your friend Mrs. Trelawney to help you with it? What is the good of friends if they do not help you, hey? You should always make use of friends, child; take that as a maxim to go through life with. Choose your friends of those who can be serviceable to you, and when you have them make use of them."

"Oh! Mr. Dysart, how you talk!" said Hannah.

"You do not like to be helped, then?"

"Oh, no!"

Mr. Dysart smiled.

"It does not do to be too independent," he said; "I am an independent fellow myself, but peste! we must give and take—do as we would be done by! And as some people find a pleasure in giving, it is our Christian duty to oblige them by accepting. Is it not so, Miss 'Annah?"

"Yes, perhaps," said Hannah, dubiously.

"But you and aunt Dess will still refuse any little testimonial or friendship's offering from me?" asked Mr. Dysart.

"I think we shall not change in our feelings about that," said Hannah, who always spoke the truth.

"Then *my* advice has no influence with you?" looking in her face tenderly.

"I did not say that, Mr. Dysart;" and she dropped her eyes.

"Well, it would be very pleasant to *me* if you came," said Mr. Gregory with emphasis.

Hannah's face was rosy enough before, but the

roses deepened in it many shades, as, impelled by quite a new feeling—something she could not understand in herself, she said—"You do not want me when you have Miss Ellen Campbell; she is far more agreeable than I am."

" The rose is not the lily, and the lily is not the violet," said Mr. Dysart gravely. "Miss Ellen Campbell is the rose, fraiche et pimpante, and ma petite amie is the violet; and a very sweet little violet she is too! I like them both; but especially the violet," with meaning. "Don't you know that, enfant? I do though, in a double sense perhaps; both the violet of the woods and the dear little human violet with the basket of tracts on her arm, standing like a fair-haired angel of goodness before me. So, chere petite, you need not be jealous," with the most superb air a man could take. "You are my little favourite of all in the Vale—you are my child-seraph—my maiden violet."

"I must go now if you please," said Hannah trembling.

" Do you not like to hear me say you are my favourite?" asked Gregory tenderly.

"Oh, Mr. Dysart! it is too strange!" said Hannah; "and I must go."

Something told her that the spasm which made her heart stop and her eyesight dim, however delicious, was dangerous if not wrong; certainly wrong if indulged in and not put away. So she turned heroically from Mr. Dysart's false lips and flashing eyes, and went down the long straggling village street in a kind of dream-waking, wherein she scarcely knew what was real and what was fancy, and whether this place of theirs was heaven and she living in unclouded bliss, or her whole life the most unsubstantial of all deliriums. And yet had he not almost said he loved her? to Hannah it meant the same thing.

She wondered why every one looked so happy to-day, and why everything was so beautiful. The most sordid colours glowed with the radiance of the sun; the raggedest children looked like Italian angels; the mean little village was as full of grace and beauty as one of Fenelon's Arcadian towns; and all life had put on new forms and new colours since the false tongue had woven its subtle lie

like a network about her. But in truth it was
with herself that the secret of the enchantment
lay. She looked so strangely beautiful in the
new emotion that possessed her, that one old
woman to whom she took her week's supply of
sulphureous godliness told her "she looked as if
she had seen an angel." And she felt as if she
had.

No person ever came to the meaning which
Hannah Marks henceforth attached to the violet; or
knew why she would sometimes blush, and sometimes the tears start into her eyes in future days
when she was teased about her "viola-mania," as
they called it; or why she asked for violets to be
planted on her grave when her last illness came.
It was the one girlish secret which she kept
sacred even from aunt Dess; the emblem of the
fatal romance which destroyed the value of her life
for ever, and withered up her womanhood into a
memory, a dream, and a regret. Ah me! what
ruined lives lie in the pathway of Love!—Love
that should be our Saviour so often our destroyer!
—Love that should be our life so often our death!

"Bon Dieu, la petite blondine is jealous! pauvre petite bécasse! la jolie chatte blanche!" laughed Mr. Dysart to himself when they parted, and he had read Hannah's heart as he would read a page of Balzac. "One is quite a Pygmalion in this cursed little place, upon my soul; and one's dolls and statues, black, white, and brown, warm into human life in the most amusing manner possible. There is not one of these little fools who would not run away with me to-morrow; even Miss Ellen with the black eyes, and half her heart given to the bumpkin. But then *she* would do it for vanity, not love. After all, what is woman's love but vanity? If her chéri is not the proudest fellow in the world, she thinks he is, and that does quite as well. No woman ever loved a man who did not in some way reflect honour on her, and no woman ever will; they are all to be bought either by gold or glory; but love, independent of vanity—bah! bah! it is a dream!" He snapped his fingers as he walked, wondering whether, if the shame fell on Aura, she would still love Jasper as she did now and cling to him to her own destruction. Gregory Dysart, and such as he, know nothing of the indestructibility of true love, and how it survives all changes and all assaults.

CHAPTER III.

CROFT was to be sold. The bills were printed and posted all over the place, and the Vale was ringing with the news. No reason was assigned; the Trelawneys were not the people to give reasons to the world for what they did; but every one felt that it was a step in some manner connected with Mr. Dysart, and that, either from personal dislike of the man (but why dislike, unless there were certain unpleasant, perhaps disgraceful associations connected with him?) or in dread of what he might reveal (and this last was the popular faith), Jasper had determined to leave the place. That stealthy evening visit of his to Gregory had become known, and the comments on it had been unsparing. Indeed, the Whisper had stopped at nothing by now; and even murder was added to the list of crimes which Mr. Trelawney had committed.

Mr. Grainger, who was still Mr. Dysart's chosen friend—that gentleman being far too clever to attempt to swim without corks even in so smooth a current as the Vale world—asked the question point blank, "whether Mr. Trelawney was not going to leave on his account? and if he knew why?"

To which Mr. Dysart made answer; "Yes, it was unfortunately too true—poor Jasper! If he, Mr. Dysart, had known that his residence at the Vale would have been the signal for the poor devil's flight, he would not have gratified his own inclination at the expense of his social status. However, the mischief was done now and could not be undone; for in honour to Mr. Lawson he must remain to take care of this pretty Lea Cottage; which, du reste, suited him so admirably for a year's quiet or so, and that book on ecclesiastical architecture so shamefully postponed. Still, it was a sad thing for Jasper, and he pitied him

profoundly; but he pitied him most for his cynical
want of trust in the better feelings of human nature,
and in his fear of a man whose kindliness and
inviolable honour towards him he had so long
proved, and therefore ought to be able to rely on,
as on a mountain rock, inébranlable."

Of course Mr. Grainger did not keep this reply
to himself; and, as was always the case after
one of Mr. Dysart's oracular utterances, the Vale
swarmed with reports like so many imps let loose
and filling men's minds with evil.

Hitherto Aura had escaped any positive scandal
against herself. She had been spoken of with
the ill-nature customary to the place, as evilly as
every one was spoken of when his or her turn
came round; but nothing very tangible had
been said of her—nothing to connect her with
the unknown crime hanging round Jasper. Now,
however, the shadow fell across her as well;
so blackly indeed, that when she went to church
on the Sunday after the posting up of those
huge bills "For sale," which had so disturbed the neighbourhood, no one spoke to her
with even ordinary lukewarmness—and few ever

greeted her with more than lukewarmness—but all looked askance; and even the Miss Campbells who had never been strong anti-Trelawneyites—Miss Ellen indeed professing rather to love her than not—yet even they, weighed down by the heavy burden of suspicion lying on all minds, to-day turned from her hastily, violently interested in the Misses Rowley and the two Misses Price—to Aura's rather haughty wonder whether it was "meant" or no. But she could not be blind to the change which had come over every one save the two Marks ladies and Harry Grant, who, as time went on and his hatred for Mr. Dysart increased with his jealousy, threw his whole soul into the Trelawney cause and made himself their warmest advocate. And he greeted Aura at the church-door, where it was the fashion of the Vale to assemble after service, with such marked respect and as it were chivalrous devotion that Miss Ellen turned quite red, distracted between two thoughts—had Harry Grant transferred his allegiance? or had she not widened the breach already existing silently between them, by taking sides with the opposite party?

It did not do her much good, poor little soul, when Mr. Dysart came trippingly up to them with his one, two, three, like a dancing-master's step— bringing up his feet quite short and close together at the end—and singled her out of the whole body for his first salutation; Harry looking on with a face rather too pale perhaps for perfect content, but else hardened into such cold indifference as Ellen had never seen it wear before, and which, in spite of her confessed flirtation with the new comer, she had no desire should be permanent.

Aunt Dess and Hannah came up to Mrs. Trelawney as she was threading the throng, leading Dotty by the hand while Julia and Mabel and Miss Tunstall followed, and spoke to her with the warmth and geniality of olden times; but save these three, and three of the "second set" too, which counted for something in the scale of the Vale's disesteem, the world turned as many cold shoulders to Aura Trelawney this bright summer sabbath morning, as there were shoulders to turn; and all but "cut" her, because

Croft was to be sold, and they were not taken into the Master's confidence why.

"Can you come up to Croft to see me to-morrow, Hannah?" said Aura. "I want to speak to you."

"Yes," answered Hannah timidly. She guessed why and about what—not having seen Aura since that fatal meeting on the road—and rather quailed at the prospect of what she had to speak to her about; but she could not refuse, and indeed would not if she could. She had not deserted her old colours so entirely as that.

"Come early, and stay to luncheon, and then you can see baby and Tiny; aunt Dess will spare you for once I dare say?" Aura continued, turning to that lady with her sweet smile.

"Certainly," said aunt Dess; "I am always glad for Hannah to be with Mrs. Trelawney." And she too smiled in that frank innocent way of hers, which made her face of fifty look like a girl's.

And then Mr. Dysart tripped up to them, heading the Campbell and Rowley shoal of muslins,

and, first lifting his hat to Aura with an inde-
scribable expression of defiance and yet of admiration in his face, he spoke to Hannah with more
familiarity than he would have used in his present
surroundings had he not wished to "show off"
before Aura, both with the grandees and her own
humbler adherents alike. Thereby adding just a
dash more salt to the brine in which the little
maid's rod was already pickling up at Croft. To
that he was philosophically indifferent. If he
could show Aura, and through her, Jasper, that
he was on the crest of the wave, and that his
word would be taken before theirs, unless indeed
Jasper would consent to the unveiling of that
hideous cancer of the past, he cared for nothing
else. Of all selfishnesses, the struggle for a place
in society, wherever it may be, is the hardest and
most cruel.

Another significant fact in to-day's strange
church-door drama, was that Mrs. Escott remained
behind in her pew waiting for the Rector; and
so avoided meeting her friends and her daughter
alike. She had heard too much not to know

how Aura would be greeted; besides, she was just as angry as the rest; and under any circumstances it would have been hard for the dear old time-server to go against the Vale, even in such a matter as the countenance of her own daughter. With some natures the first who fall away from you in times of distress and difficulty are your own blood-relations; and Mrs. Escott, like all the vulgar, was of that nature.

To-day was the beginning of Aura's social ostracism, and she knew and felt it; but not shrinkingly and not saddened. She only thought how well it was, at least for the peace of the place, that Jasper went so seldom to church; else had he seen her slighted as she was to-day, there would have been a fire lighted in that secluded Vale which would perhaps have needed to be quenched by something stronger than a woman's tears. That a gulf had opened at their feet, and that the future was beset with all manner of unknown dangers, was becoming daily more evident to her; but, with her hand in her husband's, she would either go down to destruction or fight through to the end, without fearing and without flinching. Love was stronger to her than hate or fear, and the wife greater than the conventional lady; for Aura Trelawney was one of the few women who can look through appearances and take the inner truth for what it is worth.

When Hannah went up the next day to Croft to be " talked to " she went with a certain stiffness of resolution not to be influenced against Mr. Dysart, not usual to the soft-hearted little maid whom Aura had hitherto been able to " wind round her finger," as the Valeites said. For even with her the imperious swell of the greater passion swamped the feebler freight of friendship when they came into collision : as it has done since time began and Adam was.

" Hannah, my child," said Aura tenderly, placing her on the sofa beside her, and making her take off the huge bonnet in which she all but obliterated her pretty fair face ; " will you let me speak to you as an elder sister might speak to the younger ? "

" Yes, dear Mrs. Trelawney," said Hannah,

laying her hand on her friend's gown with an instinctive timidity of action.

"It is about this Mr. Dysart." Hannah's face and neck became crimson. "My child, he is not a fit person for you to be so intimate with, as it seems you are; neither for you nor for aunt Dess; still less ought you to be seen walking with him alone, as you were that other day when I met you on the Lower Road."

"I could not help it; please, I could not," pleaded Hannah; "he would come with me; indeed I did not ask him. I scarcely knew him then—and I have never been alone with him since though I know him so much better now," she added in great distress as this new thought presented itself.

"I do not for one moment suppose that you did ask him, my dear," said Aura smiling. "I could not believe you capable of anything so unmaidenly; but at your age you should not allow any gentleman whatever to walk with you when you are alone; and you may be sure that the man who insists on doing so is exactly the last man to be permitted the grace. No man who is not very careful of the character of women is fit for women to know; and any one who would compromise a young girl is both coarse and untrustworthy."

"Mr. Dysart is not coarse," said Hannah in a low voice.

"Not in outward manner, I know," replied Aura; "but in nature he is. You are too young and unsophisticated to be able to judge of this so well as I can, from even the little that I have seen and heard of him; and certainly, when Mr. Trelawney who knows him, says that he is bad and dangerous, both I and you too dear Hannah ought to accept his verdict and believe in his judgment."

"But he and Mr. Trelawney are not good friends," said Hannah.

"And therefore my husband is unjust when he speaks of this man by his own knowledge?"

"When people are not friends, they are not always quite just," returned the girl very humbly and looking down.

Aura kissed her cheek.

"Has the poison then gone so deep with you, my child?" she said gently. "Do you too believe in this flashy stranger, of whom you know nothing, rather than in one who has lived among you for so many years?"

"Do not be angry with me, Mrs. Trelawney," cried Hannah, taking her hand in both her own and speaking with an impulsiveness very rare with her; "but it seems so natural that you and Mr. Trelawney should dislike Mr. Dysart, and yet it does not seem right, somehow, that other people should take part against him! Why should we? If half that we hear is true, it is easy to understand why Mr. Trelawney and Mr. Dysart are enemies; and yet both may be good men, though they do not like each other. Do not be angry with me if I speak honestly; I do not mean to be impertinent."

"You are right to be honest, dear; what is life worth without truth?—and you could not be impertinent if you tried; but it is also your duty to attend to the warnings of your elders, and those who know better than yourself what they are speaking of." Aura said this with a loving kind of sisterliness which went straight to Hannah's heart. "What kind of interest have I in vilifying this man?" she then continued. "What is he to me? and why should I wish to deprive you of the pleasure of his society—which in such a quiet life as yours is naturally a great pleasure—if it is not that I know him to be an unfit companion for you?"

"But how do you know?" asked Hannah, astonished at her own boldness.

"How? from my husband of course!" answered Aura.

"Mr. Dysart said he knew that Mr. Trelawney would speak ill of him," said Hannah lifting up her eyes into Aura's face, and speaking as if she was bearing her witness in the inquisition chamber, very steadily, very humbly, and very frightened. "He has told us all so."

"Because he knows that there is reason," said Aura disdainfully.

"No, not that," cried the poor girl eagerly;

"else why does Mr. Trelawney go to see him, if he thinks so badly of him?"

"My husband go to see that man? What nonsense are you talking, Hannah?" said Aura.

"But we saw him, Mrs. Trelawney! both aunty and I saw him. He came one evening about three weeks ago, when Mr. Dysart was at Mrs. Makemson's and before he had gone to Lea Cottage; and you know it does seem strange to every one that Mr. Trelawney should go and see him, and then speak ill of him, and say he is not fit to know! Shall I tell you the exact truth, Mrs. Trelawney?" she then said in great tribulation at her cruelty in opening Aura's eyes; but feeling it a duty that she should defend the absent, and if possible turn her friend's mind to the truth, however bitter, in place of being warped by her.

"Yes dear, tell me the truth," said Aura with just the gentlest shade of sarcasm in her voice; though she had been a little struck too by the revelation of that secret visit never told to her and never alluded to.

"Mr. Dysart says that Mr. Trelawney once injured him deeply, and that he knows a secret of Mr. Trelawney's which would ruin him if told; and that is the reason why you are going to leave Croft, because he has come here and Mr. Trelawney is afraid of him." Hannah spoke in a low voice, as if afraid of her own words.

"And you believe this nonsense?" asked Aura quietly.

"There is no reason for believing Mr. Dysart untruthful," she said.

"But one of us *is* untruthful, Miss Hannah," said Jasper, coming in quietly through the open door, and catching the last phrase—only the last: "either I or this man; you and the Vale have to elect which. From what I hear though, you have already elected, and have decided that the untruth does not lie with him."

"Oh, Mr. Trelawney!" cried Hannah. She was afraid of Mr. Trelawney, and did not dare to hold her own against him as she had done with Aura, whom she feared with only the fear of love not of awe.

"Oh? it is true, Miss Hannah! Because the fellow has a few foreign graces of manner, and because unfortunately for me I cannot say that I do not know him, you have all flung yourselves at his head, and have accepted as gospel any romances he has chosen to amuse you with. I tell you, Miss Hannah—I who know that man well — he is not a fit person for you to be acquainted with; and if after this warning you still encourage this intimacy, you will be culpably foolish—not only silly but criminal, do you hear? Whatever sorrow comes to you after this you will bring down on yourself, and will deserve no pity from any one. I will say no more. The girl who will not be guided by a friend's earnest prayer will not be influenced by any amount of lecturing; and if you will not attend to Aura, who is your friend, I am sure you will not attend to me!"

Hannah was silent; but running through her head, like the chords of a haunting air, were these words: "He called me his violet, and he said that I was his little favourite." Which was the same to her, as has been said, as if he had told her he loved her, and that she was in consequence bound to be faithful and true to the death. Besides, she, like all the Clive Vale world, put that one ever-recurring and unanswerable question to herself, why should they believe a man of whom they knew actually nothing even after seven years' residence amongst them, against one who spoke openly of his friends, and his past, and his place of residence, and had no secret or disguise about him? Surely the balance of distrust lay with Mr. Trelawney, not with Mr. Dysart!

"Foolish girl!" then said Jasper, his old disdain breaking through a tone of almost paternal tenderness and pity; "are you resolved on being a victim, little golden-headed moth?—and will you, in spite of all one can do or say, persist in mistaking a very foul farthing rushlight for a star, and so burn off your wings when you think you are floating up to heaven?"

"No," said Aura; "I am sure that Hannah will attend to what those who love her tell her for

her own good.   She has never been disobedient
to me yet."

Hannah looked up into the sweet face gazing
into hers with such an infinity of womanly kindness, her soft blue eyes swimming in tears; and
then she kissed Aura's hands and wrists as she
almost sobbed what was such an unconscious
confession !—

" Whoever else I love I love you, and will never
desert you, Mrs. Trelawney, or let any one say a
word against you before me ! "

" Ah, but it is love me love my dog, Hannah ! "
said Aura smiling.   " If you love me you must
love and respect *him*," pointing to Jasper, " and
believe in him against every one else."

" I cannot do that," said Hannah simply,
shaking her head.   " I know that Mr. Trelawney
is a grand gentleman, and all that——"

" But you will believe the insinuations of a
mere stranger against him nevertheless ! " laughed
Jasper a little grimly.

" No," said Hannah, " not that; but I cannot
see how Mr. Dysart is a bad man."

"Well! wait, and then perhaps you *will* see. Only let me beg of you, Miss Hannah, as you value your happiness, and your reputation in the future, keep him at a distance; do not let him become too intimate with you unless you despise the ruin certain to follow—certain to follow," he repeated impressively. "Now, wife, let us drop the subject. More exhortation would be cruel, and would only do harm. Come with me, Miss Hannah, and see my new garden in the copse; the babies are all there, and Pon is taking care of them. No, you need not put on your bonnet; we do not wear bonnets, or hats either, when we go into the garden at Croft; besides, your bonnet is ugly—it always is, Miss Hannah, don't you know that?—and your hair is pretty; and just now when a little ruffled, is very pretty; so oblige me with the beauty, and leave the ugliness for the ghosts. Come along; and you too, Aura della vita mia!" holding out his hand to his wife, with a smile as sad as it was loving.

When Hannah Marks left Croft that afternoon, if she had been asked to die for either, or any, of the

Trelawneys—I do not know if she would not have included Pon as of the number—she would have done so without a moment's hesitation. Aura she had always loved; but now she loved the grave grim Master who had spoken to her with such a mixture of kindness and lordly familiarity; she knew now what loyalty meant—attachment to her king, however much fear of the man. But she held fast by her new love too; that love without aim, without hope, without shape, that it was; and still repeated in a kind of undertone of harmony: "He said that I was his favourite and his violet."

It was with no mistrust, but rather to have nothing hidden from him, that Aura, walking up the shrubbery-walk with Jasper after having aken Hannah down to the lodge gate, said to him gently:

"Darling, why do you go to see that man?"

"Who told you that I went?" asked Jasper, with a kind of start.

"Hannah; she and her aunt, and others, saw you."

" In the evening ? "

" Yes, the evening. Why is it ? can you tell me, and will you ? "

" Will you wait, my Aura, until we have left Croft, and then I will tell you everything ? You know that I have not told you of my past life, and that I have a secret which I have never confided to you or to any one, do you not ? "

" Yes," said Aura; " I have known that from the first, but I have *felt* it only lately."

" And felt it painfully ? " and Jasper's voice suddenly deepened to infinite sadness.

" Rather," she said candidly. " It is not pleasant to feel that people have the right to suspect any evil of you, beloved. While they merely gossiped, I did not care; but I am not so indifferent as I was."

" Not shrinking, my wife ? "

She put her hand in his. " Never that," she answered.

" Wait, then; you have trusted me for six years and more, my Aura; trust me yet a few weeks longer and you shall know all."

"I will trust you to the end of time, Jasper, and wait to the day of my death," said Aura, looking up into his face; "but tell me only this one thing—does this man know your secret?"

"He does," said Jasper.

"And you are in his power?"

"In a way, yes; now ask me no more, my Aura; when the hour comes the word shall come with it."

And Aura was satisfied; at least as Jasper had said of Dysart, "in a way;" satisfied that her husband should act in this as in all matters as it seemed best to him, and satisfied that nothing he could reveal would prove him in the wrong; but haunted nevertheless with the feeling that they were on the eve of some great sorrow, and that the happiness of their lives was at an end.

This patient waiting of hers for what she believed would be their ruin, was like watching the gradual stealing on of death over the face of one beloved; and both felt that every moment was now too precious to be lost, for in how short a time might it not be that the day of destruction would come ?

As Gregory was lounging up the little village just about the time when Hannah was returning from Croft, deeply pondering over this new step of Jasper's, and what it betokened, and how he had better meet it, he fell upon the Rector and his wife walking arm-in-arm down the broad paved way of desolateness called by courtesy the High Street. Mrs. Escott was much flushed, and her cheeks and eyelids were puffy and purple, as if she had been weeping even beyond her usual tale of tears, and the Rector looked fretted and anxious, and as if the straps of his burden were galling his shoulders sorely.

" This is a sad event for you, my dear madam," said Mr. Dysart, pointing to the huge green placards staring through every shop window and posted on every dead wall.

" You may say that, Mr. Dysart," cried Mrs. Escott, her eyes getting very watery.

" And unexpected ? "

" Unexpected ! " she exclaimed; " I should

as soon have expected Corston Castle to walk down the Vale, as Aura and her children to leave Croft!"

"Do you know where they are going?" inquired the bland tormentor; "I suppose *you* do, but I think it is not generally known. Perhaps to some other estate my friend Jasper may possess?"

"I do not think that," said the Rector. The mention of an estate was a man's business he thought, which it devolved upon him to notice. For the more domestic and emotional matters, he left those to his loving spouse, being a little afraid to interfere.

"Estate!" caught up Mrs. Escott, "he has no estate, Mr. Dysart; he does not own a foot of land except Croft in all Great Britain or Ireland. One has no hold on him anyhow, not even by that."

"But he has funded property, and in a large measure?" said Mr. Dysart, with a strange gleaming in his red-brown eyes. "He used to be immensely wealthy, I know, before he played the fool as he did with his money; but even after all that happened, he had I know a considerable residue."

"And what are the funds compared to the respectability of landed property handed down from father to son, and from father to son, as long as you can count back?" cried Mrs. Escott. "If he had *that* now, one would know something more about him, and be a little more at ease. One would know where he was going to, and what he was going to do with one's children and grandchildren; as it is, he might be going to the South Pole for what one knows or can even guess."

"And you mean to say that he has not told you *that?*" said Mr. Dysart in a tone of astonishment and commiseration combined. "Ah! I pity you!—unhappy parents!—you have indeed much to bear!"

His face expressed his meaning to perfection; and its sympathy softened poor Mrs. Escott into hopeless self-bewailment, while even the Rector was touched by the genuine respect and feeling he thought he read upon it.

"You are very kind, sir," he said heartily. "We cannot but regard our daughter's marriage as a misfortune; and though I believe that she is happy, and that her husband is a good husband to her, still it is a sorrow to us all the same, and things might have been very different."

"That they might," chimed in the wife, wiping her eyes.

"I will not detain you longer," then said Gregory lifting his hat; "sorrow such as yours ought to suffer no intruder. Permit me only to offer you my respect and my deep sympathy."

He pressed their hands with much warmth, again lifted his hat with that marvellous grace, half of the military half of the dancing-master order, and turned away as if he had been speaking of a death.

"Now that is what I call a Christian and a gentleman!" said Mrs. Escott when he left them. "Never in his whole life has Jasper shown us half the feeling that this stranger has in one half-hour. Ah! if Aura had only waited for him —foolish obstinate girl!"

"She would have done better, my dear, and have had a more agreeable husband," said the Rector with a little sigh of regret.

When Miss Fitton, head milliner and appointed postmistress of the Vale, was spelling through her day's batch of letters, she came upon one in the neat half foreign handwriting of Mr. Gregory Dysart addressed to Madame Trébuchet, Rue Saint Antoine, Paris. And while she stamped it she thought;—"I wonder now if this is our fine foreign gentleman's landlady, or sweetheart— a widow may be—or may be a sister, or a cousin. I wish I could read through envelopes. This post-officing business is plaguey tantalizing ! "

If Miss Fitton had been able to gratify her wish, she would not have been much the wiser. The letter contained only these words :—

"MY DEAR LOUISE,—

"COME to England immediately. Go to Legrand's, Haymarket, where Madame de Chantreau " [underlined] "will wait until I come for her. "À toi,

"GREGORY."

Still no address, only what the post-mark might give; and still no clue to the business on hand. He was a wary old marshaller of circumstances, this well-looking gentleman from Paris; and he did not care to give even his chère petite Louise hold of a silken cord which she might perchance find it a pleasant occupation to twist about his neck. This connection with Paris was a little dangerous, you see.

So again, Madame Louise could tell M. Delaperrière nothing. She would not now if she could; not being unwilling to finger this new pie of her brother's baking, and reserving always the right of playing Judas when Judas should be a more profitable character than Pylades. Wherefore, not to be tempted, she burnt the envelope before the banker's next visit; and unconsciously —she knowing nothing of the connection between Clive Vale and the Delaperrières—Gregory was saved from instant and irremediable destruction.

CHAPTER IV.

A party at Lea Cottage!—Mr. Dysart was going to give a grand evening party! The invitations had gone out on beautifully embossed paper with lace-bordered envelopes to match, and "Mr. Dysart requests the honour" printed in violet ink; all in the finest and highest style imaginable. Had there been a Mrs. Dysart it would have been an "At Home," just to show the Goths hereabouts what the correct thing was; but this form savoured of too much lordliness of command for so thorough-bred a gentleman as the swindler from Paris; so he took off his hat and made a flourishing bow, —as beseemed him. "Dancing" was printed in the corner in a type which almost required a microscope to be legible—and the Vale knew that for once in its humdrum life it was going to have a party given as it ought to be; "the Tuileries through the small end of the telescope, as it were," said Mrs. Escott, who had a strong hankering after fine life, as a show. She probably would not have liked it in substance.

The Vale was right; Mr. Lawson would not have known his own place had he come upon it during the revels, disguised as it was by such acres of pink and white striped calico, and cart-loads of flowers and evergreens. Whatever else Mr. Dysart had or had not, he possessed decided taste, and, no matter in what capacity, had seen a good deal of the skeleton of high life; so that when he had money and undertook such an affair as the present, it was sure to be in first-rate style, and a success.

The Vale came in force. Every one in the place was there save the Trelawneys and Harry Grant; the first of course were out of the question, and honest Harry felt as if he should have choked had he broken Mr. Dysart's bread, or eaten his salt. He had not yet learnt how we have to temper honesty with courtesy in our passage through life, and how impossible it is for a wise man to regulate his social intercourse by his personal feelings. That he disliked Mr. Dysart was quite sufficient reason to him why he would not go to his "evening;" but Mr. Bennet and Major Morgan, who disliked him too, were not so consistent, and they went— under protest; comforting their anxious souls with sundry texts on Christian charity, and the need there was of not absolutely casting away a brother however erring, until he had been proved irreclaimable. All of which meant that they wanted to see Lea Cottage under its wealth of flowers and striped calico, and were by no means indisposed to such a supper as they knew Mr. Dysart would give. As it happened too, certain chance visitors were caught for the evening, who helped to swell the ranks grandly; so that on the whole the Dysart ball was what he intended it should be, the grandest event of the season, or indeed of any season which the Vale had hitherto known.

27—2

The whitest and shiniest of linen cloth was stretched over the drawing-room for the dancers— the dining-room of course was for the supper; while sundry bedrooms, and Mr. Lawson's shabby little study, and an odd box room or so, and even the butler's pantry, were pressed into the service of the evening; some made into the semblance of tents with this striped pink and white calico, and all decorated out of their original likeness and use with what was really consummate skill. The place was brilliant with light, and a select band of three—a harp, a cornet, and the piano—played the quadrilles and waltzes. In a quiet room apart were card-tables, with heaps of new packs, Janus - fashion in the court cards; and the men waiters seemed almost as numerous as the guests.

Piles of magnificent bouquets stood in moss, ranged in a jardinière in the hall; and as each lady entered she was presented with one by Mr. Dysart, who served them out impartially enough save when Miss Ellen and her sisters appeared, and to her he gave the " queen bouquet,"

as he called it—a large white mass of rosebuds
and Cape jessamine, decorated with real lace, and
fixed in a frosted silver holder; in fact a bridal
bouquet; unmistakeably bridal; and presented with
an air which said as much as words. The room
took it for a declaration; and even old Mr. Campbell, not the astutest of men, thought it par-
ticular.

"How angry poor Harry will be!" thought Miss
Ellen as she blushed and smiled and took the
bouquet half-triumphantly, half-bashfully; glancing
round a little frightened lest Harry should have
seen it all. She need not have distressed herself;
the poor fellow was safe in his desolate lodgings,
eating out his heart with jealousy while attempting
in vain to master "Chitty;" tough reading at
the best of times, but indigestible entirely to a
youth with his head on fire and his heart eaten
out with jealousy.

When the dancing began, Mr. Dysart did that
strange bit of symbolism—"opened the ball,"
whatever that may mean—also with Miss Ellen,
whom he seemed to have decided on making the

queen of the fête; and who, fluttered and proud, looked certainly pretty enough for any man's admiration—indeed more than pretty, almost beautiful. She was singularly well-dressed too, in a new white lace gown, fresh and graceful (every one in the room had new dresses for the occasion); and both she and Kate had eschewed colours for this one night, wearing white alone, with white wreaths and flowers. The effect was more pronounced than she had anticipated. It wanted only a veil to make her a bride outright.

So Mr. Dysart told her in a low voice when he was "gallopading;" adding, "I need hardly say whose bride I would wish to see Miss Ellen Campbell."

As the evening wore on and he himself became a little warmed and excited—not that he was a man to lose his head for such a bagatelle as a Clive Vale flirtation—he demonstrated his admiration even more unmistakeably; and during one of the many waltzes which they had together (he waltzed to perfection, and Ellen was the best of the Valeites,) he squeezed her waist with no very uncertain pressure, while saying to her in an ardent voice, " Bel ange ! tu ne sais pas comme je t'aime !' "

He spoke rapidly and in French, which Ellen could not follow, and the significance of which, with its familiar tutoiement, she would not have understood if she had. But the look and the gesture and the tone of voice told her quite enough; and intoxicated with girlish vanity as she might be, she thought of Harry, and the thought sobered her, bringing her up in full career suddenly. Pleading giddiness, she took refuge with Myssie, burning with blushes not to be concealed.

The Vale said it was a settled thing now; but, curiously enough it was only the elders who said this; all the young ladies, without exception all, doubted the settlement with passionate doubt, for all had certain private passages of their own which they could have detailed had they chosen, and which to them materially weakened the force of Miss Ellen's position. As for being the queen of the fête which she undoubtedly was, they said, Mr. Dysart

must have chosen one of them—the 'must' not very
mathematically demonstrated—and of course it
must have been either the eldest or the youngest;
any one else would have been too marked, and
might have given rise to suspicion, and have meant
something. It was very natural it should be the
youngest, and so of course Ellen Campbell was
chosen; Hannah Marks who was younger than
Ellen, and red-haired Fanny Rowley who wore
spectacles and was freckled but who was younger
than either, not counting.

There was certainly one in the room to whom
all this outward homage paid to Ellen, though
painful and somewhat incomprehensible, seeing
that girl-nature is much the same whatever the
temperament or yearly income, was yet only outside homage meaning nothing. Truthful and
candid, how could Hannah believe in duplicity?
childlike, how could she fathom intrigue? pure
and simple, how could she understand the gallantry of a man heartless enough to destroy a life
for vanity? When he said to her in the quadrille
(Hannah did not waltz, nor polk, nor gallope, nor

do anything but stumble through a quadrille, awkwardly as to conventional dancing, gracefully as to girlhood) : " Ma petite amie surpasses herself to-night, and looks like a seraph come straight from heaven ; " it did not make her doubtful of his truth that the next moment he was flirting with Kate, or joking with Lotty, or causing Ellen's cheeks and neck to glow with frightened blushes, as he seemed on the verge of making the decisive offer he so warmly indicated. It would have been more than she could have borne had he paid her any public attention—Semele destroyed by the lightning of her love, in very truth !

As it was, she was at times almost too happy, though at others, the first notes of a vague distress were sounding, which made her long to die. Sitting in the corner next to aunt Dess, and watching the dancers as they whirled and whisked past her in the dances she knew nothing of, what made the tears swell up into her eyes, and the great lump rise in her throat as if she should be choked ? But when her turn came in the quadrilles and country dances, when

Mr. Dysart pressed her hand, or spun her round
waltz fashion at the end, (and his arm round her
waist made her feel as if she should faint, partly
from the shame of her love and partly from the
shame of modesty,) when he told her that her hair
was like gold, and her eyes like violets, that she
reminded him of one of Guido's angels, so fresh
and gracieuse was that lovely tête d'ange of hers,
that she was like some beautiful little flower become
human—Picciola in an English dress—that he
trusted her more than he trusted any one in the place
knowing that she liked him and was his friend;
then she more than once felt as if she must have
sunk under the excess of her love and joy.   Poor
little maid! what would have become of her if she
had heard and seen him say and do the same things,
even more unmistakeable in their meaning, to
half-a-dozen others in succession?   Poor Hannah!
her initiation into the knowledge of man's false-
ness was severe enough.

In a room upstairs, practically in every-day life
the best bed-room but now a most charming little
salon, quiet and apart from the noisy dancers sat

the staider card-players. It was only a choice of
evils certainly for Mr. Bennet and Major Morgan,
for both of whom cards and dancing were equally
devices of Satan; but they chose the neighbourhood of the quieter sin of the two, beguiling the
time until supper by desultory talk with the elderly
ladies unoccupied, and languid turning over of
prints. They came for curiosity and the supper;
the one had been gratified, and when the time of
the other arrived they were content.

For it was a grand supper; such a supper as the
Vale had never seen. Champagne and claret and
strange sweet wines for the ladies flowed like
water; liqueurs were plentiful; pines and peaches
and grapes and melons and all the most delicious
fruits to be had in London, were piled up in
pyramids and intermingled with vases of flowers
down the table; crystallized fruits, gaudy crackers,
and sweetmeats of all kinds, frosted, white, and
coloured, sparkled like jewels in dishes of glittering glass; while as for the solids—no! never
since Clive Vale emerged from its pristine bar-
barism of Saxon or Dane, had it seen such meats

as what Mr. Dysart presented for the pièces de resistance of this famous supper! Now let Jasper Trelawney and he measure swords. Talk of a contest between a man who gave such an entertainment as this, and a surly, proud, uncomfortable hound, who shut himself up with his wife and children like a deposed prince for whom no one was good company enough—and the Vale thought itself fit society for kings if it could have got them—why Jasper and Aura would not have had a hand held up for them at any hour of this brilliant night! And "talk of incorruptibility!" —laughed Mr. Gregory Dysart to himself; "bought and sold and paid for, every one of them, the fools!"

In the first part of the evening the host had been too much occupied downstairs among the dancers to attend to the graver card-players above; but after supper, when the wine had warmed all hearts to a freer speed and a more generous flow, when the music was a trifle louder than heretofore, and the dancing a beat or two quicker, when the stakes had mounted from halfpenny points up to

"silver threepences" according to the Vale
vocabulary—then Mr. Dysart bounded upstairs,
profuse in his apologies for having left the
gamblers to themselves the whole of the evening.
"But not having a deputy M.C.," he said, "to
look after the young people, and not able to be
in two places at once like Sir Boyle's bird, he had
been necessitated to trust to the forbearance of
one section of his guests. And that section was
the present company." Whereat all loudly declared
that they had done exceedingly well, and that the
evening had been brilliant.

"But just to say that I have performed my duties
of a host impartially," cried Mr. Dysart, "I will
break through my rule and take a hand with
you."

He sat down to the table with his coat-cuffs
turned back, handling a pack of cards with the
extreme tips of his fingers, flirting them daintily
between the middle finger and thumb, as a
man does who is accustomed to them. His
diamond ring glittered in the lamplight, his
gold chain sparkled, his white teeth shone, and

his eyes glanced hither and thither with even more than their usual brilliancy, as he played with the cards delicately, caressing them like old friends. Then, because it was such a dreadfully bad game—such a gambling game—but merely to show them how it was played—he proposed vingt-et-un, to which they assented; even Major Morgan and Mr. Bennet—heaven knows how that was ever effected!—taking a hand for the good fellowship of the thing. They played for half an hour, neither more nor less; and then they gave up, most of them looking very grave. But Mr. Dysart rose from the table a winner of ten pounds fifteen shillings, which was to the Vale what so many thousands would have been at Crockford's or Frascati's.

It was an imprudent thing to do, but he could not resist the temptation. Gambling was his one overpowering weakness; and a drunkard could as soon have left his dram untouched as Gregory Field forbear to cheat when he had a pack of cards in his hand. Had the stakes been for nuts and almonds he would have cheated all the same.

"My strange luck!" he cried as he rose; "it is so long since I have played now, I thought it might have changed. But I am really afraid to play au serieux; I win everything before me; and you must confess, gentlemen, that is not an entirely desirable faculty."

To which a few of them gave a sullen kind of grunt, which might have been deprecation or assent as he chose to take it. And so the matter passed; and the losers had to make the best of it, sore as some of them were. Mr. Bennet was pinched in port wine for weeks after; and Mrs. Escott blew up the Rector till the poor old man, rather confused already with the noise and the lights and the champagne and liqueurs, felt as if his head was the church-bell with her tongue for the clapper; Major Morgan looked very grim whenever he thought of the affair, and was never heard to allude to it; and old Mr. Campbell and Mr. Mountain and Dr. Hale and Mr. Rowley, and one or two other gentlemen who had joined the table, being of the unconverted, wished that this exceptional luck had been theirs instead of Mr. Dysart's, and wondered how the deuce it came about. But no one suspected foul play excepting Dr. Hale, and he was too wise to speak. Mr. Grainger, who had won seven and sixpence, took the matter jauntily; and so the occurrence got itself buried decently and was spoken of no more; the gentlemen indeed being all more or less ashamed of themselves for this departure from their ordinary virtuousness.

The Vale never forgot that evening party at Lea Cottage, and for years after it was a landmark by which events were reckoned. It was the first and last thing of its kind they had known among them—the phœnix destined never to be renewed; and the next week Mr. Dysart went up to London on urgent business, he said, for an indefinite time;—" But not long enough for them to forget him, he hoped "—with his glittering smile and flattering manner.

CHAPTER V.

THE pretty little owner of the doll's apartment in the Rue Saint Antoine, no longer Madame Tré-buchet, but Madame de Chantreau for the occasion, sat in state in Legrand's best private sitting-room, waiting for her brother. Her journey from Paris to England had been after the fashion of a triumph; for at every step she had won hearts, as only minute women of fascinating manners and engaging helplessness, out a-voyaging alone, ever win them. Porters and guards, captain, steward, and passengers, English and French, had all equally petted and helped her—had all equally delighted in her sparkling eyes and dainty waist—and had all pitied the sad necessity she was under of travelling alone to see her sick sister in London, "for her husband was buried in his affairs, and her maid must be left to guard the children, so that, young and all unused to the world, she must affront the perils of the voyage without protection, trusting for aid to the kindness of her fellow voyageurs!"

Never was there such a helpless little traveller, never one so fascinating; a mere child sent forth into the world, whom it was the pride and privilege of every man to protect. She knew absolutely nothing. She did not know where to take her ticket, nor what to do with her luggage; though born and brought up in France, and speaking the French language with the true Parisian accent, you see the disabilities of her English birth still clung to her, and made her even less au courant of ordinary ways; wherefore, she cast herself on the kindness and good faith of a travelling humanity, trusting that she should be saved from total destruction.

She did not trust in vain. Everything was done for her as obsequiously as if each fellow-traveller had been her own private courier bound to render her service; while she accepted all with the gracious serenity of a young woman accustomed to be cared for legitimately, and too innocent to know that the world could make a distinction. She had the best place in the railway carriage, and her pick of the railway rugs; the captain of the Chasseurs de Vincennes made her a kind of bed, and the fat old curé wrapped up her feet with paternal solicitude; the gentleman of no profession discernible bought her fruits and delicate friandises at every available station, and presented them with profoundest homages—whereat she laughed joyously, and clapped her pretty hands together, as she lighted on a bon-bon or a gâteau of odder design or more delicious savour than ordinary.

On board the boat, to which she had been carried almost without her own knowledge and all trouble taken from her, a levy en masse was made among the cloaks and cushions and comfortable appliances of the fellow-travellers, that her impromptu sofa on the deck should be as luxurious as a queen's; and though one or two

English ladies looked at her a little sourly—
and what wonder?—yet, who minded them?
The whole male world was at her feet, (and she
took care to let them know that they were feet
worth being at) and until she came to London—
when most unaccountably she was lost at the
station, no one knowing where she went—never
did little woman with sparkling eyes and a trim
round waist travel with such an entourage of
chance adorers as Louise Field, dite Trébuchet,
Voleuse.

Only the police agents every now and then
looked in on her meaningly; news of her exit
from Paris having flashed down the line; but so
long as she contented herself with mere coquetries
they left her alone—only every now and then looking in on her just to remind her that la Loi had
still its eyes upon her, and its hand stretched out
ready for that terrible clutch if occasion served.
As it was, they were by no means unwilling that
she should escape quietly out of France where
she gave them no end of trouble, and take her
fascinating ways and nimble fingers to cette

maudite Angleterre, which, they always assert,
sends them the worst scoundrels of all—as we
say in London of them. Why should they spoil
her little comedy? they said. She was a bad
subject wherever she went, and whether in Paris
or London would have to live in her neighbour's
pockets, if not at the expense of the State—in
which it must end. Poor little wretch—pleasant
and pretty as she was, it was a thousand pities
that her father had not been an honest man
and that her brother was such a hopeless scamp;
she might have done better if well brought up; but
these Englishmen—they have no idea of the duties
of a good father of a family, and let their children run to the right and the left at their pleasure.
Wherefore, let the little wretch have her day of
sunshine while it lasted! Once cast forth on
the shores of the Perfidious, they washed their
hands of her and took no further count of her
doings.

In London, where she so cleverly slipped her
flowery chains—oh! she was a clever little woman,
the sharpest and foxiest little woman on record!—

her triumph was as entire as it had been during the journey. Legrand of the Haymarket, who always came to the hotel door to welcome his guests on their arrival and to make his adieux and many compliments on their departure, but who never saw them in the interim unless under quite exceptional circumstances; Legrand, who had a wife of his own with sleek hair and a shrill voice, likewise devoted to well-fitting black silks and jaunty little caps; Legrand, who notwithstanding his good-heartedness was as proud as Lucifer, and stood on his rights as stiffly as any Tell, knowing to a hair's breadth the exact line where courtesy slides into servility and where the innkeeper ceases to be a host and becomes a tradesman and a servant; Legrand himself superintended the comforts of this charming little woman, promising her that he would do his best to make her forget that she was in this cursed England, and that so far as his poor powers went she should still believe herself in Paris, that pearl of the world! He assigned her the best bedroom and the best parlour; and he

bade Alphonse, his smartest waiter, to be especially attentive to her, while Nathalie was to
regard madame's person and bedroom as her chief
care during her stay; in short, he and all that
was his save perhaps madame, put themselves at
the feet of the charming little woman fresh from
Paris, and who realized Legrand's ideal of the
type Parisien.

How could she resist that mobile face of hers,
so vivacious and so sparkling?—pétillante he called
it. The hair caught back in a short sharp curve
on her broad, smooth, cup-formed forehead, and
smooth and lustrous as so much silk; the fine
pencilled arch of eyebrow; the rosy lips a little
thin perhaps and loose in the lines, but fresh
as rouge de Vénus artfully applied with cold
cream could make them; the broad jaw and the
small pointed chin; the red-brown eyes sparkling
and restless like sunshine upon moving water;
the dainty feet with their incomparable chaussure;
the fairy hands with such gloves and cuffs and
rings and bracelets as only Paris can supply; the
black silk robe like a second skin; the Cashmere

shawl and the Boulevard bonnet—all sank into Legrand's soft heart like sugar into cream ; and without in the least believing " cette gracieuse Madame de Chantreau," to be anybody more distinguée than the wife of an ordinary employé say, he treated her as if she had been a duchess. " Une vraie Parisienne" he called her ; and sometimes "une Vénus de poche," when Madame Legrand was out of hearing.

He was a small fat man, this Legrand, with an acreage of back and broad round shoulders ; he wore a loose black tie under a small collar turned very low down, displaying a loose thick throat wrinkled and flaccid ; he wore also a white waistcoat, a braided coat, a gold chain, loose trousers, and low shoes ; his hands were covered with rings, but they looked rather too innocent of soap and water for British taste, and his nails were by no means impeccable. His face was smooth shaven, and he was bald and grizzled; but he was the prince of good fellows in his business, and would have retired with a fortune before now had it not been for his nationality and faith in human nature.

But while madame piled up on the one hand,
(she made out all the bills, and it is only right to
say that both items and results were simply
amazing,) he swept down on the other. For he
could not refuse a countryman in distress; and
though he would have let an Englishman die of
hunger at his door, and would have refused to
credit a Milord for five sous unless he had spoken
French and knew the intricacies of the Paris
streets, he would harbour and feed and set on
their way rejoicing, any number of stranded compatriots, solely on the faith of their fluffy hats and
Parisian experiences.

Of course he got horribly taken in; but sometimes he really did a useful kindness, and then he
was repaid, and one such evidence of honesty
balanced half-a-dozen disappointments; so, still
the fat, kind-hearted hotel-keeper went on trusting,
and swept down madame's carefully amassed piles
as fast as she built them up. She, disdainful of
his philanthropy which she called bétise and
sottise when she was angry, used to tell him
that he was not the milk of human kindness but

the butter and the fat, (which touched him on a
sensitive point,) that he was as doux as a mouton,
and with no more courage in him to say " No," than
a damp fowl; which made him awfully angry for
the time—he, who had been a National Guard in
his time !—and sent him fuming into all manner
of self-satisfying modes of revenge, which madame
would not have found perhaps so amusing had she
known of them.

But if he was kind to his compatriots—if he
would assist Gregory Dysart when he came to him
as M. Désir, a stranded Parisian whose cursed
banker had made some inexplicable mistake, and
who must be down in Wales by to-morrow's mail,
having large interest in certain slate quarries there,
and feel a renewed faith in human nature and
his system, because that gentleman had thought it
politic to repay him so soon as he got in funds,
not knowing when he might want his good offices
again—what was he to a Parisienne pur sang,
like Madame de Chantreau here ? So charmingly
ignorant of English too as she was !—for she spoke
only a few broken phrases, slowly and haltingly

like a child, so that Legrand, who had never been able to master the alphabet of ce maudit baragouinage, as he called our grand old tongue, felt himself like a Johnson's dictionary by contrast; which of itself put him into a good humour as giving him the superior place. Then she was so delightfully astonished at all she saw; delightfully not delightedly; for like a true French woman she found everything monstrous and frightful, and gave the poor Londoners credit for nothing save "material civilisation" — meaning coarse and heavy luxury; at which she tossed her pretty head disdainfully, preferring the spiritual simplicity of France, oh so many thousands of times more! that Legrand, who hated us as only a Frenchman obliged to live in London can hate the English, said it was equal to a fête-day to be with madame—almost as good as Chantilly or Les Grandes Eaux.

He took her for a Sunday drive in the park, airing his newest basket phaeton and his best horse for the occasion; and when he asked her what she thought of it—Monsieur Rosbif's culmi-

nation of public taste ?—she threw up her hands
with vivacious disdain, and called it a desert as
compared to the Bois. The statue was a horror;
the Serpentine was a ditch; the ladies were all
dolls; the gentlemen originals; the soldiers were
très bien for inches, but they looked like bûches
ardents, and the smallest little toulourou of
France was a better man than the solemnest of the
Blues; the artisans looked like beggars — were
they vraiment beggars ? — and how infinitely
preferable our ouvrier with his clean blouse and
his self-respect, not ashamed to show what he
was !—and the beggars, all in my lady duchess's
cast-off finery, were à quoi faire mourir. Where
were the bonnes ? and the neat little caps of the
" payses " out for their Sunday holiday ? Such a
mass of hideousness the little woman had never
seen !—and then they were always saying, " All
right: "—what did all right mean ?—and they were
all so triste, and in such a violent hurry: bon
Dieu ! was there an émeute or a fire somewhere ?
The streets too were so low, so monotonous, and
so affreusement ugly; the trees so withered and

brown; everything was so black, so dirty; the
sun was so pale; the atmosphere was afflicting;
and the smell of the coal smoke made her ill;
and then she branched out into praises of la belle
France, and of Paris—the queen and brain of the
world, the heart and centre, in fine the mistress
of Europe. And she talked so well, with such
delightful Parisian intelligence—that intelligence
which only a true Parisienne possesses—echoing
the innkeeper's own thoughts with such grace and
charm, that the great soft heart melted at her feet,
and Legrand of the Haymarket made the latest of
Louise Trébuchet's thousand and one conquests.

If Madame Louise had been out on any of her
marauding expeditions, instead of living en hon-
nête femme for the time being, she might have
had free quarters at Legrand's for as long as she
liked; and until madame had turned her out as
unprofitable to the establishment; which would not
have been so very far hence, perhaps; for the
busy, shrill-voiced wife did not quite approve of
her husband's sudden devotion. But inasmuch as
she sympathized with him in his longing after

France and his hatred of England, she forgave
him for the rather unnecessary zeal with which he
wore his colours on this occasion. Cette petite
madame was not a permanency, she was happy to
say; and when monsieur her brother (was he
monsieur her brother really?) came to fetch her
away, Legrand would return himself to his duties
and leave these infantile proceedings alone.
Madame Legrand was complaisante—like all her
countrywomen, and never looked too closely at
the pattern of the feminine sugar-plums which
sank into the cream of her husband's heart. She
contented herself with the bills resulting; and if
these were satisfactory, she threw in the devotion
as a bonne main—charged and paid for.

Gregory left his little sister for nearly a week at
Legrand's on principle. He had plenty of money
just now, and he thought it good policy to run up an
account at the hotel, which he would then pay off with
the grandeur of a millionnaire; thus laying a kind
of nest-egg which might bring forth the pleasant
fowl of future credit, if dark times came when the
roast was cold and the spit wanted turning. But

on the seventh day after her arrival he came up in person to redeem his pledge, and prepare for the great drama he had marked out to be played at Clive Vale.

His coming set the question of fraternity at rest; for though they were not alike apart, together they were evidently of the same mould—dark, supple, graceful, bright, lithe, crafty, cruel, sensual—something of the Hindù and the tiger and the snake and the cat, all in an inextricable entanglement of resemblance together. Legrand heaved a sigh of content when he saw them embrace, which they did after the French fashion in all formality, he kissing her forehead only ; and madame was not quite so content perhaps ; though why she should have grudged a casual lodger an affectionate brother who paid his bills like a lord, might have puzzled her to answer satisfactorily.

"Pauvre chatte ! tu as souffert !" cried Gregory; suffering being a respectable commodity in certain aspects. And when he had said this, the innkeeper and his wife withdrew, and left the pair alone.

And when alone, Madame Louise, laying her hand on her brother's shoulder, said in good clear English—

"Why, what on earth is up, Gregory? You look, my! what a swell! as if you had carried off old Delaperrière's bank on your back. What have you been about?"

"I have fallen into luck, Louise," said Gregory, smoothing his moustaches; "into such luck as even your keen brain cannot conceive of, and that your best-laid schemes could not come near. Guess! I will give you three guesses—I will give you a dozen, and you will not find out. Now, fire away —number one: what is it? and who is it?"

"La, Gregory!" simpered Louise; "I daresay it is some of your horrid gambling tricks again!"

"Miss the first. Not a bit of it! no gambling: by Jove though, I did the neatest thing the other night! I will tell you presently; but no gambling; no clever likeness of signature—fancy old Delaperrière being so sharp!—no walking into wrong rooms; or mistaking between the gold watch unpaid for, and the small trousse honestly discounted; nothing that can bring me into unpleasant relations with messieurs of the law; and you must own that is a luxury in itself, petite, worth a great many days of trouble!"

"Indeed, it is!" she sighed, thinking of her late relief and the banker's offer.

"Well! my find is a good, tractable milch cow; looks like a lion but is only a cow; with a yield, as the farmers say, that will feed and clothe and pay for all our little pleasures, petite, from now to the end of our lives, if we are careful."

"What can you ever be driving at?" cried Louise. "You were always such a funny fellow, Gregory! Don't you remember how poor papa used to laugh at you? I am sure you must speak more plainly if I am to understand you: you know how stupid I am."

Brother and sister looked at each other on this, and laughed—below their breath. They were speaking too below their breath, having a wholesome fear of ears laid against key-holes—where theirs would have gone if there had been anything they wished to hear—and the consequent discovery

of their little farce of nationality. But they spoke
in English because they did not wish to be understood in what they said if overheard, and they
spoke in a low voice, hoping that it might pass
for German.

"I have found some one," said Gregory; "some
one that we have lost for ever so many years;
some one whose recovery is our fortune, and if you
manage your part well, from whom we can get a
settlement for life!"

"Gracious! what are you talking about?"
exclaimed Louise, opening her eyes to their
fullest; which she seldom did; "who do you
mean, Gregory?"

"Carthew!" said Gregory.

She gave a little scream and covered her face.

"Mon Dieu!" she said, startled for the moment
into a natural voice.

"Yes," said Gregory tranquilly, "Carthew;
and through you, Louise, the fortune of the
Fields!"

"I declare Gregory, you quite frighten me!"
cried his sister looking up; "you look so grave,

as if you had such a tremendous thing on hand!"

"So I have, ma sœur; and it is a responsibility I almost dread, that of trusting it to your manipulation. If I did not believe in your entire devotion to my wishes, and in your fraternal instincts, I should hesitate gravely. But I am sure I can count on my little sister, and she on me."

When Gregory wished to be impressive, and when he was particularly false, he always spoke in a kind of translated French; which Louise understood.

"Certainly," she answered; "my brother may rely on me. Where does Jasper live now?" she then asked, settling herself into a business-like air and attitude.

"At a place called Clive Vale," answered Gregory, watching her.

"Clive Vale? where is that?" she asked. "I do not remember such a name in the geography book we had at school."

But she did know the name; she had spelt it out on the post-mark of his last letter; but she

wanted him to believe that she had not spied after
him, even in so small a matter as this; and
Gregory, who was always taken in by her when
she chose that he should be, thought that the
stamp had been blurred.

"He is living there however; is married, and
has three children."

"And les chères petites, Julie and Mabele?"

"Are with him; grown quite handsome girls—
would make a sensation in Paris. They are like
us, dark and graceful; not large, but taller than
you—at least Julia is already—and Mabel will
not be petite; they are well-mannered, and look
nicely brought up; the madame there is a superb
woman, and knows the best form of English life."

"Pauvres petites!" murmured Louise; "I
should so like to see them!"

"You shall; that is just what I intend."

"Merci, mon frère," she said simply, as if that
was all.

"He is no longer Carthew," Gregory went on
to say, smiling at his sister's little transparency.

"No? what then? Has he changed his name?"

"Not exactly; but he has dropped the surname; he is Mr. Jasper Trelawney now, and no one knows him by any other. Remember this, Louise; it is a fact important to be remembered."

. "I understand," she said; "continue."

"He is married, as I tell you, under this name. His wife and her family know him by no other— have no suspicion that there is another—no one in the place has; but they all suspect that something is wrong with him, because of the profound silence he has kept on his past life—a silence so profound that it has challenged suspicion."

"Just like him!" said Louise; "he was always si peu diplomate!—so proud, so sensitive, and yet so weak in the way of management; he could never arrange anything! As if the mere brute silence was enough in this world!"

"The old tactics; and this time bringing him to ruin," said Gregory. "No, not quite to ruin, because I am merciful; but very nearly so; might be quite if I willed it; as it is they have only brought me, and you too ma sœur, a fortune for life."

He looked at her keenly.

"I confess I cannot see my way yet," said Louise looking down.

"Then listen; I would have you go now to this Clive Vale—now, during my absence."

"Oh!" interrupted Madame Louise innocently; "then this is where you have been all this time?"

"Certainly; where else? and how else could I have fallen across Jasper again? But I will tell you the story afterwards. Go there then, now, during my absence as I said; it would not do for us both to be there together, as you can understand, for you see I do not wish to be mixed up in this matter publicly. Go to the lodgings I shall indicate—to a Mrs. Makemson's——"

"What a horror of a name!" again interrupted Louise, taking out her ivory tablets and gold pencil-case to write it down.

"—— Live there with extreme care and caution; go out from between the hours of eleven and one, which I have ascertained to be the hours when Julia and Mabel walk with their governess; meet them, speak to them, embrace them, weep, say nothing in any way to commit yourself, but use many affectionate expressions; do this often, but not more than this; see no one else; speak to no one else; if gentlemen or ladies of the place should call on you—they might, but I do not think they will—refuse to see them. Jasper of course you must avoid as you would avoid the devil; do not go to church; give Mrs. Makemson no kind of hint as to who you are; and above all, remember you know nothing of Mr. Gregory Dysart, Rue de la Paix, No. 15. Do you see the drift of what I would have you do?"

"Perfectly," said Madame Louise: "you wish to frighten Jasper——"

"Into a settlement of five hundred a year."

Her eyes sparkled. "On whom?" she asked.

"On me," he answered carelessly, "to keep you buried."

Madame Louise said nothing; but the "cat and the chestnuts" came into her head, and trotted there for the rest of the interview.

"You deserve your good fortune," she said

aloud very sweetly, "and you may rely on my doing all I can to help you. I understand your plan; tell me only how I am to get to this Clive Vale—by what train and at what hour—give me money, for I am "—she flung up her hands with a French expression in the gesture, and then she said in English—" cleaned out," without mincing, "and je suis à toi, mon frère," laying her hand in his.

He pressed it tenderly. " Chère petite chatte," he said in a natural voice, " tu es bien bonne ! "

" But for all that I will have a few chestnuts for my own roasting," said Madame Louise to herself; "and if I can make a better thing of it by flinging you over, Master Gregory, you will be flung over;" and while thinking this she raised her bright brown eyes to her brother's face, smiling affectionately and saying aloud; " we were always good comrades and true friends; we can trust each other, n'est-ce pas ? "

"Mais oui ! " he answered caressingly. Then he suddenly exclaimed—" By Jove ! I had almost forgot ; you must be in mourning, Louise."

"I have none with me," she said; "and I cannot wear English patterns."

"What folly! half the effect will be spoiled with colours."

"Not at all, my brother," she answered in a hard, dry tone; and Madame Louise could be like iron when she chose. "Colours suit me, rélevant the sombreness of the black robe; and I absolutely refuse to wear the clumsy English dresses. You know I understand *that* art, at all events."

"Would you spoil the whole game for a piece of feminine vanity, little fool?" cried Gregory angrily.

"I must dress as I think best, and as a lady does dress," she returned coldly.

"You would wreck the best-laid schemes of a life for that cursed love of finery of yours," cried her brother. "I thought you had more sense, Louise, and understood business better."

"It is because I understand it so well that I am firm," she answered. "If you had wished for mourning, you should have told me in time, and I would have fitted myself out in Paris convenablement; but nothing you can say will induce me to wear an English gown or an English bonnet, come what may, Gregory."

"But why? diantre! tell me why!" said her brother.

"Because they are ugly," replied Madame Louise; "and I do not like to be ugly."

"Are you going to Clive Vale with any ulterior thoughts of fascination?" asked Gregory sternly.

"Not at all, my brother; I am going quite simply, but as I think it best to go. You may drop the subject, mon cher. I am willing to give you all the help I can, as you know—for of course all this is for your good, not mine, excepting in so far as your bounty may make me a participant;" this she said in the smoothest and softest voice, without a shadow of the cats and the chestnuts in it. "But for all that I cannot consent to make myself a fright, even for mon frère."

"But there are French dressmakers and milliner creatures in London; ask Madame Legrand," urged her brother.

She tossed her head disdainfully. "And look at madame's cap! I could tell at a glance that those coques were made by inferior fingers. They say that they are French, ces petites cochonneries who come over here; but what are they?—little couturières who could not earn ten sous a day at home, and so come to London to set themselves up as grand milliners from Paris. No, thank you! I know my métier better than that!"

"You are as obstinate as ever, I see," said Gregory pettishly.

She gave him a sharp look, and her thoughts flew back to the portly, well-dressed, middle-aged man who came to see her sometimes in the Rue Saint Antoine; but she smiled sweetly and answered meekly; "I am a rock in the matter of caps and bonnets, if wax in all else."

And Gregory knew there was no help for it; the uncompromising little woman would have her own way as she said, "coûte qui coûte."

"And now for your story," she said, when this little tiff had cooled down again. "How did you find ce pauvre bon homme?"

"By the merest chance, consequent on unrelaxing search. A paradox, hein?—yet a truth. You know I have never given up looking for him, and I always knew I should find him some day; so when that Delaperrière business failed, and I had to cut for it, I came to England; in bad plight enough, but Legrand here, good old soul! helped me with money; more than ever resolved to consecrate myself to the discovery of Carthew. Had it cost me my fortune, instead of giving me one, I should have accomplished my design. Fate did not torment me long. As my initiatory step I went down towards Wales, where I have a large slate quarry somewhere in the clouds," smiling, "working the line as I went—at least meaning to do so. The first place I stopped at was this same Clive Vale, where I found that Fortune had placed loaded dice in my hands. An old fool, conceited, shallow, and soft as butter, a Mr. Grainger"—Louise looked up at this, and still with her tablets in her hand quietly wrote down that name too—"spoke to me after church was over; I took his measure like lightning—it was inspiration, Louise!—got into his confidence; learnt who were the inhabitants of the place; and among others heard the name of 'Mr. Jasper Trelawney.' This was enough. I searched farther, and soon made out that he was my man. Conceive my feeling at falling upon my aim so soon! I went up to his place next day; saw him; frightened him out of money by threatening to tell his real name, and how he had married under a false one, &c., &c.—also threatened to blow the story of his alliance with us; which was what his pride could not bear as I had anticipated. He gave me money at the moment, and sent me more by the evening to buy me off. I had old Grainger with me, by chance you know, as witness; and voilà!—do you not see? I was endorsed at once as known by Mr. Trelawney, who could not contradict any report I might choose to make of myself, because he had put himself in my power. I have lived on him ever since; and as Mr. Gregory Dysart am one of the first people of the Vale. I have taken Lea Cottage, and live en grand seigneur, but I don't spend much money—I have not much to spend, good as the catch has been." This he said for his sister's benefit.

" Make any ? " she asked.

" No ; I never play ; only the other night ; but that I will tell you presently. To our story."

" Tell me first ;—are there bonnes fortunes or steady ones for you there ? "

" Neither, 'pon my soul."

" No affaires and no money ? "

" None ; only the gentlemen have fortunes at Clive Vale—the ladies not a rap. There are one or two single men with money, but the girls——" he snapped his fingers in the air.

" Continue," said Louise veiling her eyes.

" Well, beside my threats and the hold I have on him by his change of name and all that Paris business, I find by a hint thrown out, 'pon my soul! in the most masterly manner, that he *knows* nothing of that Funchal affair; so of course he will be ready, if dexterously handled, to pay anything to burk such an uncomfortable fact as a dead wife turning up again to claim him.

Don't you see? Do you fully understand what
I mean?"

"Yes, yes, perfectly," she replied. "I know
the lay as exactly as if I had gone through it all
twice over. Now tell me about the people of the
place."

And Gregory did; and almost without intend-
ing it let his sister into his whole design, of how
he would establish himself either at the Vale or
at some other remote English village, as one of
the residents for life, marry pretty Ellen Campbell, and become a respectable man at last. But
though he included his petite sœur over and over
again in his scheme, Madame Louise said afterwards it was only as a bead upon the thread, not
as an integral part of the net. And again she
thought; "If I can make a better settlement for
myself here or in Paris, I will do so, and Gregory
and his precious plots may go to the wall, and
stick there for me!"

Louise was so far the cleverer of the two that
her brother believed in her, and saw only what
she chose he should see. And yet he did not

tell her that Madame Delaperrière was Patrick
Grainger's sister; though he told her everything else, and gave her the social map of the
country with photographic exactness, not flattering.
Neither did she tell him that M. Delaperrière,
banker, had called on her more than once, and
had bribed her to betray him.

CHAPTER VI.

WHAT had come to Clive Vale? or rather, what had gone out of it? The sun was as bright, the fields were as green, the woods in their early autumn colours were as gorgeous, and the hedgerows as gay with flowers, as ever; but the place was changed to the perceptions of all, and as if the life of society had departed. Visitable humanity was limp and languishing; and now that Mr. Dysart was away, the exotic amusements which he had so carefully planted among them, faded like the flowers of that "garden sweet" when the fairest creature who tended them like her own children, died.

The archery field was deserted save by the younger three Misses Campbell, who, wisely re-

membering the day of the future when there
would be more ties to shoot off and more prizes
to win, thought their time not ill employed in
practising ; they also kept up their croquet—and
they alone ; but the doll's boats were abandoned,
" laid up in ordinary," said Miss Lotty a little
pertly, when Mr. Grainger asked her and her
sisters to go to the lake and float them with him,
seeing " no fun in going with that stupid old
fellow, with his ridiculous manners." And
indeed even the croquet and the archery practice
had been matters of duty and common sense
rather than of pleasure, being dull in comparison
with what had been. The horses, in imitation of
Mr. Dysart's, were turned out to grass ; and Mr.
Grainger had never been so glad to get rid of anything in his life as of his Roman-nosed brute with
the one white stocking, who nearly pulled his
arms off with a mouth as hard as iron and a neck
as stiff as a poker. He was too much of a
countryman not to understand a good horse when
he saw him ; but he like all the rest, and he more
than all the rest, put his eyes in his pocket

when the question was of Mr. Dysart's knowledge, and was willing to take on trust whatever the other chose to offer. There might be refinements in horseflesh he thought, of which he was not aware; as there might be refinements in everything; and by that "might be" Mr. Dysart had ruled the Vale world.

Dreadfully dull was the place this week, and all at once too. Nothing seemed stirring, and the young ladies were spiritless and fretful to an extraordinary extent. Suddenly all work-baskets overflowed with needlework which it was absolutely necessary to sit at home to do; and arrears of reading and visiting were to be made up with as little delay and as brave a conscience as possible. But though no one acknowledged it, not even sisters to each other, yet every one knew what ailed every one else, and why there was such a sudden outburst of home-feeling, and such smiling congratulations "on the nice quiet days we have had lately, when we have got through such a quantity of work!" The augurs of Rome were not the only people in the world who could not talk of their mysteries together without laughing.

Beside the home rents and rives so assiduously mended, the two Misses Price sought consolation in a fierce resumption of their parish duties; and all the old women who for the last few weeks had been left in quiet possession of their sins and themselves, were suddenly whipped up again with double lashes—the one representing time lost and the other favour to regain. They went back though to the fold with troubled consciences; knowing that they had been coquetting with wolves outside; and thought the fare poor and the shepherd harsh. They felt that they were not forgiven; though Mr. Bennet was too vain not to clank the chains of his recaptured prisoners, sounding them in all market-places that the world might know what captives he had, and how he held them. Still, it was conquest and not friend-ship; captivity, not fraternity; and both they and their young master knew that it was but a Carthaginian peace, to be broken again at the first opportunity. At present however, he was in the ascendant, and not that other; who, like all the absent, was in the wrong whenever the question was of comparative values; but Mr. Dysart's absence and Mr. Bennet's coolness made the Misses Price feel as if all the late past had been a tremendous mockery—a mere phantasm and delusion, which they had followed to the destruction of their peace. They had been so long in the narrow Calvinistic groove, that it was not wonderful if they felt their late aberration even into the mild worldliness of which they had been guilty, as a sin needing atonement and by no means undeserving of punishment. Had any permanent good come of it, that would have been a different thing; but as it was—now that Mr. Dysart was away, they returned to Mr. Bennet and his ferule and their chains, and were glad to make the best of their condition.

To all outside appearance Hannah Marks was the least influenced by the Dysart eclipse; the young ladies thought she had least cause. She had not lost what the others had lost; why then should she mope as they moped? Mr. Dysart

was very kind to her, because he was so kind to
every one; but of course he made a distinction
and did not treat her as he treated them. She
was a dear little thing, and they were all glad
to know her and be kind to her and all that,
but she was not quite of their own set, and
Mr. Dysart understood that. So they reasoned in
secret among themselves, when discussing with
closed doors and in the strictest confidence, who
they thought liked Mr. Dysart best, and to whom
he was most affected. And of all on whom they
reasoned, Hannah Marks was the one put farthest
out of court.

And yet what ailed the little maid? Very pale
and wan and listless had she become of late, doing
her household duties as diligently as ever, certainly,
but doing them with a strange kind of apathy
quite unusual to her. It was not that she com-
plained, that she flinched, or that she forgot; not
the smallest of the thousand little niceties of attention which she had accustomed herself to perform,
and aunt Dess to expect, did she lay aside; her
weekly cake was baked with the same scrupulous

care, and surreptitious delicacies were still prepared
for aunty, whose appetite was poor and had to be
tempted unawares; her flowers were still watered,
and her table bouquets made; she dusted the
drawing-room; she looked to the silver and glass,
and gave the forks and the tumblers an extra
polish; she ironed the fine things, and she made
aunty's caps and collars as good as new; but with
all this accuracy of fact the spirit had departed,
and it was only the ghost of her former life that
poor little Hannah was leading now.

The change had been gradually coming on her
for some time; indeed, ever since that day when
the crafty tongue and the flattering eyes had bap-
tized her into an illusion, and she had given up
her heart for a lie and an hour of frothy flattery.
And when she saw Mr. Dysart drive past their
house on his way to the station—driving himself in
the pretty little pony-carriage he had bought, and
looking like a prince as she thought—the vague
distress which had been growing for so long —
growing since the establishment of the archery
society to which she was not admitted—growing

larger since Mr. Dysart's removal from Mrs.
Makemson's to Lea Cottage, by which indeed she
seemed to have lost part of her very life—growing
since the flattering speech which had struck the
poison into her—that vague distress culminated
as with a piteous cry, she fled away heart-broken
into her own room, and burst into those bitter tears
of the young who love unwisely.

Mr. Dysart had looked up as he passed, and
kissed his hand gallantly; lifting his hat and
smiling, as if the sight of the little pale face turned
shyly to him had been a pleasure he cared for;
throwing into his glittering eyes an expression
which said as plainly as words, "I am grieved to
leave you chère petite, and shall be rejoiced to
revisit you." And she had this look to carry next
her heart as a precious memory to cheer her till
the hour of her timid joy should strike again.
But she grew paler and quieter day by day, and the
blue veins showed more clearly, and the purple
rings about her eyes deepened and enlarged, and
the dimpled corners of her mouth went down, and
over her whole being was cast that indefinable

shadow, that sorrow without a name, which tells the anxious looker-on that a girl is breaking her heart for an untold love.

But the young ladies of the Vale put Hannah Marks out of their calculations altogether when they were discussing among themselves by whom Mr. Dysart was most missed, and who seemed to be his favourite. For the last, they all agreed on Miss Ellen Campbell; censuring her at the same time for her sin in captivating two men at once.

Aunt Dess was as much at fault as the rest. It never came into her gentle mind to suppose that Hannah could be in love; she would have been surprised if such a thing had happened, even under the legitimate circumstance of leave demanded and granted for the wooing; but that she should have fallen in love with any one unasked, on the strength only of a few whispered compliments and a little seductive by-play, was to her as inconceivable as if the girl had committed some most grave offence against the received canons of morality. No; Aunt Dess read consumption in her face and thinning figure—her mother had died of consumption, Laurence had not had a very strong chest, so that there seemed to be a reasonable ground for fear—but she read nothing else, and applied to Dr. Hale secretly, not wishing to alarm her niece to whom "the doctor" was a formidable man. He sent her horrid strengthening draughts of steel and quinine, and "bitters" for her appetite; but tonics and strengthening draughts do not touch the heart; and Hannah's cheeks lost their roses as steadily as before, and the purple rings about her eyes deepened and enlarged, un-touched by steel or bitters.

During this time too the Grainger and Bennet feud got more force, and blazed out in fresh fires, spluttering and hissing but not leading as yet to any social conflagration; only expressing itself in small bickerings and spiteful encounter of wits, Mr. Bennet having now the whip-hand, and galling the poor captainless lieutenant savagely. In fact, every one was in a bad humour; as was but a natural reaction after so much pleasurable excitement; and some were on the stool of repentance as well.

Among these was pretty Miss Ellen Campbell,

doing penance for her late disloyalty; for Harry
Grant by no means intended to let her off easily,
being himself uncertain how far she had been
only flattered, and how far really won. And his
was one of those honest natures, with just so
much of serviceable sternness running through,
that disdained all double-dealing whether in love
or hate, and made him able to cast off the chains
of the most beautiful enchantress that might be,
when once fairly convinced that she was Vivienne
and not Elaine. He had sundry griefs against
Miss Ellen. That she should have made herself
so prominent as a " fair Toxophilite " was one of
them; and that she should have won, and what
was worse, have worn the Palais Royal bracelet
was another, and a large one; that she had entered
into all the Dysart amusements with such girlish
enthusiasm comprised many griefs in one; but
that the world should have the right to point at
her as the favourite, perhaps the chosen future, of
the man he hated and distrusted, was beyond a
grief—it was the beginning of a tragedy. That
grand evening party to which all the Vale had

gone with brains turned upside down, and whence
he had excluded himself with the sulky fidelity
to his creed characteristic of him, but of which
he had heard such distracting accounts of how
beautiful Miss Ellen looked, and of Mr. Dysart's
"marked attention"—that grand evening party
was like the first draft of the deed of separation,
which it seemed to poor Harry was about to be
signed and sealed between them; and when he
met Ellen and her sisters to-day, returning from
the archery-fields where they had been practising
—(he noticed though, that they were in every-
day costume, the Toxophilite livery abandoned for
the time being, as there was no one to captivate)
Ellen, all crimson blushes and bashful eyes of
penitence, was the last to whom he spoke, and
her hand was the one he took most coldly.

But he turned back with them, as he had been
accustomed to do; and walked on the outside next
to Lotty, between whom and himself had always
existed the frankest and most romping friendship
of all. His status was different with each of the
three sisters. He was Myssie's boy, Lotty's romp,

Kate's brother, and Ellen's lover; but the world, which judges only by the outside, would have assigned him to Lotty who used to pull his hair and slap his face when he was saucy, and who once gave him a right good uncompromising kiss at Christmas time, when they played forfeits, and he stood in the middle of the room with a candle in his hand, while Miss Lotty was bidden to go kiss the candlestick as her punishment.

Ellen was a little jealous by nature, and always inclined to be jealous of Lotty, who however, much as she liked young Harry, would not have married him if he had asked her; at least she thought not. Perhaps the asking would have opened new vistas and developed new feelings. And to-day when Harry, who was on such bad terms with herself, went round to the romp's side, and began talking with such unembarrassed pleasantness, the black-eyed coquette's jealousy flamed up mightily; and had Mr. Dysart been at Clive Vale Harry would have had a bad time of it. It was fortunate for both of them that he was away, plotting against the peace of others, not of them.

As it was, like Ariadne abandoned by Theseus, she was defenceless, and Harry Grant was master of the situation. Lotty was not ill-natured and not inclined to dispute the field with her young sister; so, after a time, she and Kate slipped themselves in leash and walked off in front, in that wonderful way in which girls manœuvre when they like—outdoing the best-trained veteran in the army for the neatness and dexterity of their movements. Thus the two sulky ones were left together, to rend or heal the breach already existing between them.

For a time they walked on in silence, Harry too much moved to speak and Ellen too much offended; but finding that her temper was only punishing herself, she thought she might as well try the other tack; so, looking up shyly, she said—

"Are you coming home with us for croquet, Mr. Grant?"

"No," said Harry a little bluntly. "I have no time, thank you."

"I thought I heard you say to Lotty that you were coming," observed the young puss, fibbing shamefully.

"Miss Lotty did not ask me," answered Harry.

"Oh! then, no wonder you will not come! You would if she had; of course I did not expect you would for only *my* invitation."

"I do not think I have always made that distinction," said Harry, his voice just a little softened. "I think I have always been the proudest to obey *your* wishes, Miss Ellen, whenever I have been honoured with them." Which was an immensely courtly speech for Harry, who rather despised courtliness as "French" and "unmanly."

"What a pretty speech!" laughed Ellen; "you have been learning to compliment, Mr. Grant."

"It has become the fashion at Clive Vale," answered Harry. "Compliments seem to be beating truth and feeling out of the field of late."

This was a home-thrust, and Ellen felt it.

"Why should you think so?" she asked with enchanting innocence. "I do not think that truth and feeling are ever beaten out of the field, as you call it."

"Oh yes, they are!" said Harry bitterly.

"English honesty has no chance against French flattery any day!"

And then there was silence again, for as long a space as before.

"How busy you seem to be now!" Miss Ellen said, when the pause had become too awkward to be borne longer. "You have no time for anything."

"I have time for all my duties, Miss Ellen," replied Harry, who seemed bent on making himself disagreeable; "but I have no time to waste on amusements."

"Amusements are not always waste of time," said Ellen archly.

"Has that been your experience of late, Miss Ellen?" exclaimed Harry quickly; pouncing down upon her like a hawk on a hedge-sparrow.

She blushed violently, and did not answer. She was not particularly clever at anything, and not at all quick at repartee.

"If all one hears is true, Miss Ellen, it has *not* been time wasted with you," Harry went on to say, almost choking with his words.

"I do not know what you mean, Mr. Harry," she answered, playing with her bow.

"Well, it is not time lost, I suppose, when a young lady makes a conquest of such a man as Mr. Dysart," said Harry, steadying his voice as well as he could; "and gives him her own heart in return," he added with emphasis.

"Who has?" she asked, still playing with her bow and twanging the slack string nervously.

"You have, Miss Ellen."

"I am sure I have not!" she cried with energy.

"Every one in the place is talking about it," said Harry.

"I thought you knew better than trust to the gossip of Clive Vale!" she pouted.

"Then you are not in love with him?"

"With whom?" she asked, looking down; she knew the words were a challenge, and meant them to be so.

"With Mr. Dysart," said Harry, his heart beating.

She tossed her saucy head. "I am not the girl to fall in love quite so easily, or with a man

who has never said he loves me," she answered;
her answer cutting both ways. "How can you
believe such nonsense, Mr. Grant?"

"I am only too happy to disbelieve it, Miss
Ellen," Harry exclaimed warmly.

"How you hate poor Mr. Dysart!" she then
said. "What has he ever done to offend you, I
should like to know?"

"He has destroyed the comfort of the place,
and he has made you cool to me," answered Harry
boldly.

"He has made *you* cool to *me*, you mean,"
cried Miss Ellen impulsively. "Why you
scarcely ever speak to me now, and we used
to be such good friends!"

"I am not changed, Miss Ellen; it is you,
not I."

"I am sure I am not," she said, turning away
her head.

Harry stopped short in his walk, and took her
hand. "You are not playing with me?" he
asked, anxiously looking into her face.

She was silent, biting the end of her glove.

" You are not changed to me ? "

" No," she answered hesitatingly.

" You do then love me, Ellen ?—you do ? "

He pressed her hand till she nearly cried out with the pain, for Harry was something of a rough wooer, and translated into practice his text of truth and honesty.

"I did not say that," said Miss Ellen coquettishly, and a little frightened now that it had come.

" Oh, do not trifle with me ! " cried Harry, all his soul stirred as only an honest man's soul can be stirred with love. " Tell me frankly now, once for all, do you love me or not, Miss Ellen ? I did not mean to ask you till I could ask your father too—till I could keep you as you ought to be kept; but I have been so miserable lately, I have been driven out of my resolution I scarcely know how ; I know I am doing wrong—but, dear Ellen, tell me, do you love me ? "

"I thought you knew that long ago," said Ellen almost in a whisper, turning away her head but leaving her hand in his.

" And you will wait to be my wife ? "

" Yes," she said gently ; " if you think I can make you a good one."

Harry, saying something wild about heaven and angels, threw his arms round the girl—for all that it was in the high road—and kissed her ; and, as he held her pressed to him, he said in a coaxing voice—

" You will be good now, Ellen —now that you are mine—and not flirt with this fellow any more ? "

" Of course not, you silly boy ! " said Ellen ; " how could you be so ridiculous as to think I ever cared for him ? "

She did not tell Harry how he had squeezed her waist in the waltz, and called her his " bel ange." Neither did she herself know how much this action had had to do with her decisive coquetry of to-day ; for Ellen, if somewhat feather-headed was true-hearted, and did really love handsome Harry all along, as she phrased it ; though she had been flattered, of course, by Mr. Dysart's princely homages. So much flattered indeed, that she had become afraid of herself and of him ; not in the least desiring to find herself some bright day demanded of her father, and caught in an engagement. Naughty little flirt as she was she did not want to be taken seriously, and lost to bright-eyed penniless Harry Grant for ever. A rival is sometimes a man's best friend, when the woman has sense and loyalty enough to be afraid of herself.

But now Harry had got himself into a dilemma. Happy as this chance meeting had made him— what was he to do ? He dared not ask Mr. Campbell's sanction to the engagement; for if there was one principle in life which that worthy old gentleman held unflinchingly, it was his determination not to allow his daughters to enter into long engagements. Most fathers have some crotchets about their daughter's marriage; and this was Mr. Campbell's. But on the other hand, it went against all Harry's own ideas of honour and integrity to have a secret engagement un- known to the family and hidden from the world. Englishman-like he hated intrigues of all kinds, and thought concealment cousin-german to false-hood; so what between his love, which now included certain duties and obligations to Ellen —his honour, which was his self-respect and good conscience—and his knowledge that an explanation would close the door against him until such time as he could knock at it with a sufficing income in his hand—Harry Grant was troubled in his mind, and perplexed exceedingly as to the path he ought to take. Like many wiser and stronger men he waived the immediate decision, and parted with his betrothed in the vague hope that "some-thing would turn up," which helps to tide us over the first of a difficulty by giving us time to collect our forces for the real strain.

When they got home, Ellen, following Kate her bosom friend and confidante into the bed-room, sat down on the bed and began to cry.

"Why Ellen, child, what is the matter with you?" cried Kate, going up to her and kissing her. "Did you and Harry Grant quarrel?"

"No," said Ellen, looking up through her tears and laughing hysterically. "He made me an offer, Kitty, and I have accepted him ; and so we are engaged."

"My goodness ! " cried Kate ; " how angry papa will be if Mr. Dysart makes you an offer, as I think he will !   He will never let the engagement go on.   Why Harry has not more than a hundred a year now.   What shall we do?—and what will the boys and Myssie say ? "

" I don't know, Kitty ; I have been a great goose perhaps, but I could not bear his being so cool to me.   I am afraid I brought it on a little myself," she added half-penitently, half-ashamed.

" You naughty girl ! " said her sister ; " how could you be so imprudent !   That comes of flirting with two at once, Ellen !   I have always told you you would get into some dreadful scrape if you were not more cautious."

" But I do love Harry Grant," cried Ellen with energy ; though she began to weep afresh as she spoke.   " He is so handsome and so good ; he is such a darling, Kitty !   Isn't he now ? "

" He is a very nice boy indeed," said Kate

warmly; the Misses Campbell always called him boy—they called most young men so—a habit caught of their brothers; "but I do not think papa will let the engagement stand, and then there will be such a fuss in the place! Every one will know all about it, as with that horrid Dr. Hale; and you will be so uncomfortable, Ellen. However, we cannot help it now, so we need not look on the black side of it. Wash your face in cold water, child; here is my rose water; and for goodness' sake don't let Myssie or Lotty suspect anything. Keep it a secret as long as you can; you will only get into trouble if you do not."

So spake youthful wisdom to youthful imprudence; and by the aid of cold douches, dabs of rose-water, and the ingenious fiction of a headache, Ellen's flushed cheeks and swollen eyelids escaped too searching observation; and when Lotty asked Kate, "Did Ellen and Harry quarrel to-day?—Ellen looked as if she had been crying;" the only answer she received was: "Did she, poor little thing? Not that I know of."

CHAPTER VII.

———◆◇◆———

" PAPA, the place is bewitched ! " cried Mrs. Escott, bursting into the study where the Rector sat making believe to read Mosheim with shut eyes and open mouth and nose unmistakeably sonorous.

" What is the matter now, my dear ? " he asked, rousing himself in the brisk way in which people do when caught at untimely napping.

" Why, as if we have not had enough of plots and mysteries already, lo and behold, a foreign lady must needs come to the place now ! I never saw anything like it—people drop down upon us as if they came from the moon, and one has no sooner done with one thing than another turns up. Now who is this woman, I should like to know? and what is she doing here?"

"I am sure, my dear, I cannot tell you; and very likely we have no business with it at any time. Where is she?"

"At Mrs. Makemson's."

"And what is she like?" asked the Rector with a man's natural curiosity.

"She is very pretty, I hear, beautifully well-dressed — all these Frenchwomen do dress so well!—and lives very retired, scarcely ever going out, and doing a quantity of embroidery. She has been a week there, papa, and no one has known anything about it, so just fancy how close she must keep!"

"Who has told you about her now?" asked the Rector.

"Jane; she is Mrs. Makemson's niece, you know; and she went down to her yesterday evening—it was her Sunday out—and there she heard all about her. It is most extraordinary! I am sure my poor head gets quite bewildered, it does, with all these queer things happening. I feel all going round with them."

"Sit down, my dear," said the Rector; "I hope it is not apoplexy."

"I am sure I should not wonder," said Mrs. Escott. "If it was apoplexy, or typhus fever, or anything, I should not be surprised. One has no peace in one's life now, and I am getting quite ill with all this excitement and mystery. I am not used to it, papa; and it does not suit me."

"No, my dear, it does not," said the Rector soothingly; "and I wish it could be different for you."

He took the wind out of her sails cleverly, and stopped the blame she was just about to throw. For somehow, everything that went wrong in Mrs. Escott's life was due either to her husband or her daughter; not because she did not love them, but because they were the things handiest for a blow when her temper was up; and it was seldom down, poor yeasty soul!

So now the fact was oozing out in the Vale that a strange lady had taken up her quarters at Mrs. Makemson's, where she sat at the window all

day long—behind the window-curtains though—
going out with unvarying punctuality between the
hours of eleven and one, but at no other time;
and also that she was pretty, well-dressed, a
beautiful worker, sorrowful, ladylike, and—with a
secret. "Secrets again! they were never going to
be rid of them!" said Mrs. Escott petulantly,
when speaking of the occurrence to Mrs. Price,
who merely answered, "No; since Mr. Trelawney
married your daughter, Mrs. Escott, a blight has
fallen on Clive Vale"—thus touching the poor
lady on her tenderest point, and humbling her
into a proper state of self-abasement — a state
considered by Mrs. Price as ineffably salutary for
every one's soul but her own.

The only people who knew nothing about the
lady—who did not even know that Mr. Dysart had
temporarily left the place—were the Trelawneys.
More and more withdrawn from the social life of
the Vale, as the circle of love and fear was closing
round them—shunned by all more than they had
formerly renounced for themselves—they knew
nothing of the gossip rife below, and almost as

little of the events. Save when Mrs. Escott went up with her windbag which collapsed at Jasper's touch, and when Hannah let her small modicum of news escape her, Aura had heard nothing. That was because she would hear nothing. There were plenty who would have told her all, if she would have allowed them; but she imperiously forbade the subject of themselves to be discussed before her; and if, when she paid her morning calls which were her only means of visiting, Mr. Dysart's name was mentioned and the conversation began to flow in his direction, she used to get up to take her leave, so resolute was she to know nothing but what her husband chose to tell her of his own free will. Which was not much, as we know; the time not seeming to him as yet ripe for confession.

Wherefore, they were entirely ignorant at Croft of the fact which the whole Vale was beginning to know, that a pretty little Frenchwoman, by name Madame de Chantreau, was living in a kind of half-hiding at Mrs. Makemson's, or that she went out between the hours of eleven and one regularly, no one knew where or for what. Apparently though, to no good result for herself; for Mrs. Makemson used to notice that when she came in she looked weary and disappointed, and would fling herself in the easy chair in an attitude of as much despair as fatigue ; sighing frequently, and sometimes wiping her eyes—which presupposed tears as of necessity.

So much though of the life of the place did they know in their airy cloisters, that they were aware Hannah Marks was failing in health. Aunt Dess had told Aura so in a note which accompanied the return of some books she had lent them ; and Aura, who really loved the girl, was grieved, and thought what could she do for her ? and how could she help her ? Nothing better presented itself at the moment than to send down the children with some fruit, and flowers, and amusing books, and Berlin wool patterns, and a sheetful of crochet, and specimens of tatting, with other small womanly devices to kill time pleasantly; adding a note to aunt Dess and Hannah jointly, saying, that if they thought so

small a change as " up to Croft " would do the
girl any good, both she and Jasper would be
charmed to have her, and would do their best to
make her as happy as a princess in a fairy tale.

People have strange notions sometimes of what
does, or ought to make one as happy as a princess
in a fairy tale; but Aura was at the least retro-
spectively right in her formula; for if Hannah
three months ago had had to ask a boon of Santa
Claus, it would have been an invitation to Croft.
Now perhaps it would be a less perfect delight;
for though no personal coolness had fallen between
her and Aura, yet they stood in opposite camps,
and one was an enemy where the other loved.

Aura had nothing to do with this; and though
Mr. Dysart was seldom out of Hannah's mind—
colouring the whole of her existence—he was never
in hers save in relation to her husband, and when
obliged to remember him. So she sent off her
family to aunt Dess—the dog, the donkey, and
the panniers; the babies, the nurse, Miss Tunstall, Julia, Mabel and Dotty—"all the foolish
things together," said Jasper with a pleasant

kind of humour—he was never bitter at home—
with permission to return by a longer round,
for the sake of the walk and the lovely day.

It was early when they set out—almost an hour
before their usual time; so that when they went
up to Miss Marks' door, the dark little woman at
Mrs. Makemson's had not gone yet on her daily
ramble, but was sitting with her bonnet on,
putting the last stitches to a slip of " broderie à
l'Anglaise," with which she designed to make the
Vale ladies jealous when she lifted her gown to
show her ankles and her petticoat. She had no
need to ask who they were. Julia and Mabel she
recognised, both from likeness and description;
and her heart beat faster as she saw them, so
like her former self! — memories of the time
when she was as young and unscarred by the
brand of sin rising up like mournful ghosts before
her. Not that the impression lasted; nothing
lasted with Louise Trébuchet save her appetites,
her vanity, and her love of money; but it is
something to touch, if never so transiently, a
heart grown hard and stiffened in iniquity.

Sitting behind those famous flowered damask curtains of Mrs. Makemson's, where her brother had so often sat and played the spy before her, she watched the unconscious family party, and even heard their voices and what they said. She saw aunt Dess and Hannah both come to the door, and Miss Tunstall and the elder three children go into the house with them, carrying their baskets of flowers and fruit; she saw the babies kissed and petted, baby proper shutting his eyes and opening his mouth as if lips were things to eat, and kisses suggested dinner, while Tiny shrugged up her wilful shoulders, and said, "Na! na!" as usual, holding out her hand to the nurse with as much injured dignity as disapprobation on her rose-red, lovely, sulky little face; she watched the whole pretty comedy of the nursery—that shifting picture, bright and innocent, so dear to all women—with something of a woman's delight but with more of a woman's envy; but the sole intelligible comment to herself was: "Elles ne sont pas mal mises, les petites—il faut que cette madame soit assez convenable!"

Then the visit came to an end and the children streamed down the town; the people turning out of their houses to look at them, as they always did whenever the Trelawneys "showed," which was not often. And as they turned the corner, out of her own sight, Madame Louise skipped downstairs and followed them.

It was easy to follow them—she called it " guetting them "—for they walked slowly, the donkey not approving of violent exercise; and when clear of the town, they took up much time in picking flowers and running after butterflies; besides, Miss Tiny then insisted on her rights, and would be taken out of the pannier to walk under pain of such an uproar as would have justified legal interference; so the little woman, carefully keeping them in sight while apparently absorbed in reading a limp, flapping, yellow pamphlet of huge size and coarse illustrations, was in more danger of falling on them before her time, than of losing them. At last they turned up a lane which led by a round to Croft, but into which a pathway through some cornfields took foot-passengers, by a short cut, sooner and higher; the same cornfields as those through which Jasper and Aura had walked that blessed summer evening six years ago.

The little woman from Paris knew this way by heart now; as she knew all the ways which could in any manner be made to bear upon Croft. As soon as they turned up over the bridge, she dashed through the small swing gate, and hurried along the path till she struck the road again. Then she turned down the hill, and walked leisurely; but looking about her as one a little perplexed. In a few moments she heard the children's voices; then they came in sight; and now she met them face to face.

They all stared at her in that stag-like way of astonished children, Julia and Mabel almost absorbed, and looking half-entranced; for a strange lady unexpected, on their own roads, was a greater event than a strange gentleman; men having a wider roving commission all the world over.

"Pardon!" said the lady in a clear, flute-like voice, speaking with extreme precision but with a strong foreign accent. "I am a stranger here, would you have the goodness to direct me to High Cross? I think it is High Cross," looking into some ivory tablets clasped with gold and studded with rubies, which hung from a châtelaine at her side.

Miss Tunstall, who of course undertook the office of answerer, entered into a full explanation of all the stiles and lanes and gates and rights and lefts, necessary to find the special group of cottages going by that name; and while she spoke, the lady, still attending to her and acknowledging her instructions by " Oui, madame," " So," " Je comprends," and other small evidences of assent, quietly and smilingly took a hand of Julia and Mabel each, and drew them nearer to her.

Then, when the governess had ended, bowing her thanks graciously she turned to the two little girls, saying—

" Parlez-vous français, mesdemoiselles ? "

They laughed and blushed and fidgeted and looked at each other; but on Miss Tunstall's " speak, my dears," replied shyly—

"Oui, un peu."

"Whee!" said the lady, correcting them with a strange manner of familiar right, but kindly—as a mother would correct her children. "Whee!—comme ça, nette!—pas wee. Pardon, madame! perhaps you are Madame Trelawney, and I am impertinent?" she said interrogatively to Miss Tunstall.

"No, I am not," answered that lady with a merry smile; while the children laughed outright at the idea of "Tunny's" being taken for Mamma; "I am only the governess."

"Ah! je comprends!" said the lady.

Still holding a hand of each of the two girls—still drawing them nearer to her—she stood looking at them with a changeful face; a face expressive of intense emotion sought to be subdued. But presently the struggle became too great; her emotion mastered her strength. "Chères petites!" she cried with a sudden outburst of passion, flinging her arms round them, and wildly weeping. "Mes jolies petites anges! mes chéries! enfin je vous revois! Ah! you do not

know me, nor what cause I have to love you!
Pardon, mademoiselle! but the sight of creatures
so dear to me, so inexpressibly dear, has stirred
me and opened my soul! And you do not know
me!" weeping afresh, "you do not know me!
Ah, mademoiselle! what it is to love the dearest
things one has in this world! ah! if you knew my
despair!—if you could read my anguish! Mes
enfants! mes enfants!"

As she uttered this cry she covered her face
with her hands, her slight lithe body quivering
convulsively.

Is there such a thing as natural instinct?
What then was it that made Julia and Mabel
incline to the lady lovingly, while Dotty stood
with his hands in his pockets staring defiantly?
Never had the two girls felt as they felt now for
this strange lady kissing them and weeping over
them; and they longed to tell her that they loved
her, and to ask her to come home with them and
live with them.

Poor Miss Tunstall was terrified at the whole
occurrence: sure that something was wrong, and

that she would have black news to take up to
Croft ; but still she knew that she was not to
blame, nor could she have prevented anything that
had happened ; not even when the lady said, a
little calmed from her grievous agitation : " will
you rejoice to see me again, mes enfants ?—will
you see me lovingly?" and the children pressing
closer to her answered fondly, " Yes, we will."

" Now you must do me a little grace," she
said ; " you must wear these for my sake. I have
had them made for you express ; see, they are
pretty and they are not nothings ; they are fit
for you to wear, chères enfants, croyez-moi ! "
She drew from her pocket a French jewel-case,
from which she took two little gold lockets, each
attached to a fine gold neck-chain. The lockets
had a forget-me-not in turquoise on the back, and
in the inside was a feather of raven hair, fine and
silky as a child's; faced by an inscription, " à ma
Julie " on one, and " à ma Mabelle," on the
other, with " L. C." below.

" Your mother's hair," she said, clasping them
round their necks. " Will you wear them in

her memory, mes enfants, and think of the poor
lady who one day met you, and told you her heart
was full of love for you ? "

" Yes," said the children putting their hands
into hers, and of their own free-will kissing her;
while Miss Tunstall's gentle " You must ask your
mamma, my dears," evaporated into thin air, lost
to all ears save her own.

Then the lady kissed and caressed them again
—shed tears over them and called them her
children, her treasures, her chéries, and her own
long-lost little angels, and wrung her hands as if
in despair when the moment of parting came,
and she must absolutely abandon them—looking
back when she had finally torn herself away, with
a long and tender look, waving her handkerchief
for as long as she could see them. And so they
passed out of sight—the two girls utterly bewildered but in a torrent of excitement; Miss
Tunstall in tears and trembling; and the servant
maid, who had not understood half she heard,
but who, by reason of her status and her Sundays
out knew more of the Vale reports than did the

governess, with a firm conviction that Master
had been a "bitter bad villain" to some one
—but whether to this fine foreign lady or to
missus at home, she had not quite made up her
mind. Meanwhile, Madame Louise Trébuchet
went back to the village tranquilly, congratulating
herself on her success and manner of acting; and
the two girls broke away from the rest and ran up
the hill, in their eagerness to get home and tell
the story of their adventure.

Jasper and Aura were sitting in the quiet
sunless noon beneath the horse-chestnut tree;
where indeed they had been almost ever since
the children had gone out; enjoying as even
the most devoted parents do enjoy the temporary
absence of their young ones, when they become
lovers again, uninterrupted. Not that there was
much enjoyment in the Croft life now. Love as
tender and trust as firm as ever stood between
them, but the gloom which overshadowed Jasper
was repeated in Aura's sadness, and the Fear
which made life a burden to him, almost too
heavy to bear, found an echo in her dismayed

ignorance of the real nature of the distress which had come upon them so stealthily and suddenly.

They were talking now of what they would do when they left Croft, and where they would go; Jasper not having made any decided plans for the future, possessed as yet only by the blind instinct of escape; and both were inclined to a residence in London — Aura feeling, and he knowing, that if any one wishes to be " lost " that is the best place in the world to be lost in—except perhaps New York, from which both revolted.

" Wherever it is we shall be together, and that will be enough ! " said Jasper passionately ; " enough for me if in a desert, Aura, so long as you were happy and content."

" I do not think it would make much difference to me where I lived," Aura answered. " Home is not the four walls we hang about with pictures and curtains, but the love, the honour, the faith, we live with."

" And that you have yet for me, is it not so ? "

said Jasper with a wistful air; "not chilled, not
faded, my wife? the full summer warmth still
rich and living?"

"Not fallen into the autumn yet, darling," she
said smiling. "I am not quite old enough for
wrinkles or grey hairs, still less for that terrible
heart-chill of age; and I shall never be old enough
for that to you," she added, leaning over him fondly
and drawing her hand caressingly over his eyes.

"Are you sure, wife?" he asked, holding her
hand over his eyes and pressing the cool fingers
against them.

"Yes," she said; "sure as of my own existence,"
and looked at him lovingly. "Women who love
truly do not change," she added; "we have one
love for life—one love only, Jasper—even under
the appearance of change; men are different, are
they not?" and she laughed.

"Sometimes," he answered; "a man *can* love
twice."

"*You* could not?" and she kissed his hand:
whenever Aura loved her husband with most
entire love, she kissed his hands or his eyes.

"I could love no one after you," he answered.

"But——"

"Now!" and he put his hand over her mouth. "You are a true woman in that, wife, that you must look back, and must dig below the roots."

She laughed. They were so happy to-day! it was long since there had been such a full chord of love and peace and serenity between them; some of the late cold shadow of fear seemed to have been lifted from them—as when the sun comes out after the threatening of the storm has passed.

"It is something to have lived and loved," then said Jasper in a half musing voice. "That wonderfully deep saying, 'Ich habe genossen das irdische Glück—ich habe gelebt und geliebet,' is true of every living soul that has loved. If even love is slain by death, and happiness is quenched in tears, still to have loved is priceless gain; and the past is as true as the present."

"Sometimes truer," said Aura, not thinking of themselves. "When the greater love has been abandoned, and the lesser accepted, the past is then truer than the present, inasmuch as intensity is truth."

"As it would be to you," he said, "if you married any one else."

"Jasper!" she cried, "how can you talk so! Do you think I could love any one but you, and am I the woman to marry where I do not love?"

"Women do sometimes," he answered.

"Not good women," she answered a little severely; "only a few poor miserable weaklings, taken by their vanity, or their compassion, or their weakness, or their ambition, or something that is not love and that ought not to be marriage; but not a woman who knows herself, and who has as much will as I," and she smiled.

"No, I do not think that you would marry again if I were to die," said Jasper.

Her eyes filled with tears.

"If you were to die," she said in a low voice, "I suppose that I should live for the sake of the children; but I should never know a day's happiness again. I might get to peace, but not to happiness. Oh, Jasper! life would not be life without you! I should live as one without a heart or soul—as a mere machine—a mere animated skeleton!"

"You would not live," said Jasper; "you and I could no more live apart, my wife, than the earth could live and bring forth her harvests without the sun. We are wedded for time and for eternity—for life and for death," he put his arm round her waist. "Is it not so, my Aura? You would not—could not—leave me under any circumstances?"

She smiled incredulously.

"Leave you! what on earth could make me leave you, darling?" she said. "Leaving you implies free will, my own voluntary action. Well!—I might be driven to commit suicide, but I cannot contemplate it as a possibility."

"No test would warp you, then? are you quite sure of that?" asked Jasper feverishly.

He often put this kind of question to her now, like a man consumed by doubt which needs perpetual assurances to soothe away.

"Sure," she answered steadily; "I know that I have to be tried in some way; you yourself have told me so, and I can see and feel it; but I cannot imagine any circumstance whatever that could happen to us that would have the power to chill or change me to you. Whatever the past may have been, the present is mine and sure!"

"Keep it yours—keep it yours," cried Jasper, in the same feverish way; "let nothing take it from you, Aura; whatever happens, be greater than circumstances, be stronger than fortune!"

At that moment they heard the rapid pattering of the children's feet.

"Oh, mamma! papa! we have seen a lady!" cried Julia and Mabel, rushing across the lawn and almost unintelligible from haste and eagerness.

"Gently, gently, my darlings!" said Aura smiling. "We cannot understand you if you speak so fast; and how heated you are, children! Where are Miss Tunstall and the babies and Dotty?"

"Oh, we left them miles behind!" panted Mabel; "and Julia and I ran all the way home to tell you. Look, what she gave us!" and they held out their lockets. "Look, papa! Such a pretty lady, and spoke half French, and was like some one we have seen somewhere and we cannot recollect who. Are they not pretty?"

"But who is the lady, and what does it all mean?" said Aura bewilderedly. "Come, sit down children, and tell us what you mean! Papa cannot understand a word of it all, and I am sure I cannot!"

She looked at Jasper as she spoke. He was sitting with his elbow on the arm of the seat, his head leaning on his hand; he was pale and rigid, his burning eyes alone showing life or emotion; but his features were set, and the hand lying on his knee was clenched and strained. And then the Fear fell for the first time on Aura, and she saw the shape of the evil haunting them.

"She was a very small dark lady," began Julia; "not so tall as I am, and spoke strangely—half in French—and her English was odd and not like ours. She met us just by the stile going into the cornfields, and asked us the way to High Cross, I think; and then she asked Miss Tunstall if she was you, and she spoke to Mabel and me, and

began to cry, and called us her enfants, and kissed
us very much.   And then she gave us these
lockets with poor mamma's hair in them, and
said we were to wear them for her sake ; and that
she loved us, and we did not know her, or know
why she loved us.   Oh, mamma ! she was so nice !
I wish we could have her here !   She was so
pretty !—so pretty !—with such lovely black hair
and dark eyes !   And such dear little lockets !
Look, mamma, mine has 'à ma Julie ' in it and
L. C., and Mabel's has Mabel—Mabelle it is,
though.   Who is she, mamma ?   Papa ! do you
know who she is ? and why did she cry when she
spoke to Mabel and me ? and why did she not
take any notice of Dotty or Tiny or baby ?
Mamma, who is it ? "

"I cannot tell you, my dears," said Aura in a
low voice, stroking Julia's hair while Mabel
spread herself over her lap, kneeling on the
footboard and looking up into her face.   "I have
not seen her, so I cannot tell."   She could not
speak much, her voice was failing her and her
lips seemed stiff.

"Don't you know, papa?" persisted Mabel; "she knew us, so she knows you. She was not tall like mamma; she was not so tall as Julia, and with such black hair! and oh, such small hands; mine are much larger than hers! Papa, who is she?"

"It sounds like a fairy tale," said Jasper speaking with an effort, "and I cannot answer you at once. Suppose you go into the house now; I will talk to you about it afterwards."

"May we wear our lockets, mamma?" asked Julia.

"Yes," said Aura, her lips quivering; "if papa likes."

"Not for a day or two, little girls," said Jasper slowly.

They both spoke so unlike themselves in voice and manner, that the children looked at them wonderingly, understanding nothing.

"Come Julia, let us go and show them to nurse," then said Mabel, who soon got impatient of gloom. And they ran off in the same tumult and fever as they had been in ever since Louise

Field dite Trébuchet had met them in the road, and kissed and cried over them.   .

Jasper and Aura sat for a few moments silent; then Aura turning to him and fixing her large eyes upon him steadily, said very quietly, but in an altered voice ; "Jasper, tell me, were you legally married to the mother of these children ? was she your real wife ? "

" Yes," said Jasper, covering his face.

" Your wife, Jasper? your wife ? and before me?"

" Hush, hush, Aura !" cried Jasper, clutching her to him ; " you are my wife, only you !   She is no wife of mine now."

" Is she divorced ? " whispered Aura.

He made no answer.

" Tell me ! tell me ! " she said urgently ; " did you divorce her ? "

" No," said Jasper.

She gave a piteous cry and flung herself on her knees—

" My God, my God, help me ! " she said, holding up her hands to heaven ; and then letting her face fall upon his knees, she burst into a passion of tears—such tears as few of us are, mercifully, permitted to shed—the tears of the woman who has lost her all! "And I who love you!" she sobbed; "she cannot love you as I do, and yet she is your wife!"

"She is not my wife, Aura," said Jasper in a low voice. "Who are you speaking of? a mere phantasm, a delusion, a passing stranger, coming no one knows whence or how. Will you give me up so soon? for a mere word—a fear?"

"I will give you up for nothing so long as I may hold you," said Aura, looking up through her tears and kissing his hands. "But if I may not—if another claims you——" again she buried her face against his knees, quivering.

"You hold me for life," he answered almost sternly in his strength of will; "and I hold you and will not let you escape."

"No! no!" she cried, weeping bitterly; she was too much broken now to control herself; "I do not hold you; I am not your wife."

Just then the voices of the little ones coming up the shrubbery drive struck upon them.

"My poor children!" she exclaimed. "Oh, Jasper, why have you done them this wrong? No!—I did not mean to reproach you!—beloved man! my own husband! forgive me that I did! You are great and good and true and loyal; I know that you are loyal; but my poor little children!—my brave boy, shamed for ever——"

Something in the thought overpowered her. What the woman and the wife had borne, the mother could not. Her face blanched suddenly as a spasm struck through her heart; she gave a heavy sigh, and murmuring, "Take me home," sank fainting on the grass.

"If it is true," said Jasper half aloud, as he bent over her to raise her, "I would that she were dead now at this moment, before fresh anguish comes upon her!"

But she was not dead. Strong hearts live long, even under as heavy a weight of sorrow as hers, and none of us can say when the moment of ineffaceable despair has come.

CHAPTER VIII.

"No answer, ma'am," said the servant, bringing Aura a minute pink note, highly scented and addressed to "Madame Trelawney, E. V.," in a fine pointed hand, very small, and with immensely long tails to the letters.

"No answer?" she replied.

"No, ma'am; the lady said we were to say no answer; she left it herself at the lodge," replied the footman, looking, trained as he was, as if he would have liked to say more; but he read no encouragement in the pale stately face before him, statelier than usual and with even more than its ordinary womanly dignity upon it; for what dignifies so much as love and sorrow nobly borne?—so, as a kind of official relief to his

feelings, he shook out an unoffending anti-
macassar and laid it straight on the chair again,
and then left the room. If it had been winter h e
would have stirred the fire.

Aura was sitting in the library, the only room
in the house sacred from the children, still pale
and broken but calmer than she had been.
Jasper had been with her all the afternoon, talking
of the day's occurrence; having now got the full
account from Miss Tunstall who had not been
too much frightened to use her senses, and who
repeated as accurately as is possible to an inaccurate
humanity, all that had occurred. But he had
gone out now for a few moments, the men in that
eternal copse needing him; so that when the note
was brought in she was alone, for which perhaps
she was almost thankful. She did not wish to
distress her husband again, and she did not know
how far she could as yet trust herself. She opened
the note with that cold deliberate courage of
despair, and read—scarcely comprehending what
she read—'Louise Trébuchet de Chantreau's
words.

" MADAME,

"I IMAGINE that children as well elevated as these of yours—and mine—will not fail to tell you of my meeting them to-day. I shall be in despair if I have brought sorrow to your house, but I was impelled by the love you can understand so well, to come and see for myself beings so dear to me as these chères petites. I had heard—n'importe où—that their father, who I once knew so well—too well for my peace, moi, malheureuse !—was living here, and I, not wishing to see him or to distract you, madame, flew here to the children; I wished to see them unknown to them, to speak to them gently of their poor mother, and to leave them these two little souvenirs of her love. But I did not wish to be discovered. The agitation I was in betrayed me, and I lost my head, as other women in my pénible situation would have done. Pardon, madame! but you have a so much finer heritage of the two, you can afford to be generous to a pauvre femme comme moi, a beggar for love where you are a queen. You have *his* love, my children, and your own; you have money; and I am as deprived of money as of love! No longer loved by the one man I would have given my life for, childless, poor, destitute, living from day to day not knowing where my next crust may come from, do not be angry with me that I have looked in on your paradise, and the sight of my pale face well known, once beloved and now abhorred—oh my heart! that word!—has disturbed his peace and yours. I have often wanted bread since *he* left; and I have now had to trust to the kindness of the only friend I have in the world, to lend me money for my expenses here. Yet if I had had to sell my very robes I must have come to embrace my beloved children. I do not ask you for anything; but I think madame you will feel with me, that I ought not to be left in this poverty, and that it would be only becoming in your ('my,' was scratched out, but left quite sufficiently legible to be seen) husband, if he were to make me an allowance. Standing in the relation which I maintain towards him—the father of those dearest little ones, and they, my own flesh and blood, so well protected and cared for, and dressed like les petites princesses, and elevated to so high a station—is it just, madame, that I should be destitute ? Two hundred a year out of your funds would not be so much, and I would then go and hide my poor head in some obscure corner of the globe, and would trouble your peace no more. You would not desire that I should appeal to your mother, or to any third person, as an advocate on my behalf, a sympathetic arbitrateur for my rights ? Yet you are aware perhaps of what my rights are, by laws both of France and of England. But I would not wish to speak of cold, legal rights. I would wish to support myself on the larger and nobler sentiments of your heart and of his. Do not fear that I shall create confusion and suspicion here at your house by an unfortunate identification of name. I have long abandoned my right appellation, not wishing to be reminded of lost happiness, and a home destroyed and deroofed ; I am not Mrs. Carthew—how sweet the name!—which of course you are aware is *his* true name ; but Madame de Chantreau, to which du reste I have a right by my mother. Thus, madame, I can neither say that you have usurped my name, since you are known only as Madame Trelawney; nor can you m'en vouloir for shocking against yours, even though I should be in my right, and you—in an illusion.

"In conclusion, I again ask you to reconsider this question of the allowance. He used to be generous, and at one time would refuse me nothing. Ah! men change, madame! it is only les femmes who remain constant! I am about to leave this place, having now accomplished my design, and having seen with my proper eyes these beloved children, for your care of whom I would wish to thank you, madame, very gratefully. Thus, any interview sought either for you or for him would be futile. I will see not him nor you. If French by habit of life, I am English in loyalty. Adieu, madame. Pardon me, and in your happiness and fruitful being think sometimes of the griefs of an unhappy woman, whose great crime was that she loved, and who has been generous enough not to destroy your happiness, when it lay at her feet to do. If you have any communication to make to me, and wish to show the sympathy of a woman with a woman's trouble, send me a commissionnaire, and I shall receive your epistle before leaving. Pardon all faults of style. It is rare to me to write English letters. Suffer me to embrace my children once more, and suffer me again to thank you for your care of them. A mother can understand those thanks!

"I have the honour to remain, madame,

"Your devoted,

"L. DE CHANTREAU."

What should she do? She sat with the letter open in her hand, and thought. But turn which way she would, the future looked dark and full of trouble to the poor wife who saw herself threatened in the tenderest part of her life—to the mother who had sinned against her children so grievously and yet so innocently! Not that she intended to accept all this as undeniable till proven; so much had her conversation with her husband taught her. But at the best—taking it at the best as a rogue's plot—it was a tremendous position; while if true, it was simply death or the disgrace of a life. Jasper would still be Jasper to her; the one sole love of her heart; the father of her children;— do men understand the full force of that?—her beloved; but not her husband, that sacred name second only to that of GOD when coupled with true love. But losing that name, what would he not lose of integrity in her life! The love that is hallowed by marriage is so dear to women; and marriage itself, with the home, the matronhood, the honour, the safety, the dignity resulting, so precious, that the unloved (not the unloving) wife seems more an object of envy to them than the loved mistress, and most would choose the former state rather than the latter: unless of the school which has shaken itself free of fetters; of which Aura was not.

While sitting thus, pondering, Jasper returned to her. She put the note into his hands silently, asking only below her breath:

"Is it her handwriting?"

"It is like it," said Jasper, trembling as he

glanced over the page ; " a little changed perhaps, but it is the same in general appearance."

Aura covered her face with her hands, and the tears slowly forced themselves through her fingers while her husband read the letter, word by word, as if painfully spelling a lesson. When he had finished he laid it down, and taking a low chair came and sat close to her side.

"I see she has told you of my change of name," he said ; " the secret which I have kept from you for so long, and which I did not wish to tell you while we were here. However, you shall know all now."

" Then, you are not Jasper Trelawney ? " she exclaimed, looking up and pushing the hair from her face as if heated and confused. " Is it all a dream ? is it all going to fade away ? " she said dreamily, as if speaking to herself; for in truth, she had not understood that paragraph. Beyond the mere fact that another woman claimed Jasper as her husband, and the children as her children, and took credit to herself for generosity in leaving Aura her home and her family, she knew nothing. She was too much stunned to enter into details.

"I am, and I am not, Trelawney," he answered steadily, holding her hand; "though for all that I am a true man, and your husband, Aura. I am, as she says, Jasper Trelawney Carthew; but I have dropped my surname, and will never resume it—neither I nor the children."

Jasper knew what that nervous pressure of her hand in his meant, when he said this; some of the children had no right to any name of his, should this terrible thing be true; and Carthew, or Trelawney, it was all one to them!

"Shall I tell you my story now, my Aura?" he then said, still holding her hand; "are you strong enough to listen to it? It has nothing very sad in it, though much that has wrung me and made my life worthless and withered—utterly so till I saw you, my wife! and the springs of love and happiness flowed afresh. Shall I tell you?"

"Yes," she said, "let me know everything now; the time has come for the truth without reserve, whatever it may cost either of us to hear it!"

"The beginning of the wrong lay with myself alone," he began. "I ought not to have married her. I did not really love her, and I knew that I did not; but I had become entangled, and—the old story of false honour! I thought it better to fulfil my engagement and marry, no matter what the warnings of an unsatisfied nature, than to break my word on what seemed to me the pitiful plea of not loving so much as I knew I could love. She was young, pretty, engaging, and simple; not very wise but pleasantly childish in manner, and light-hearted enough to gladden even so grave a man as myself. She was partly foreign, having been brought up in France; and I could see for myself had many points about her confirmatory of her own account of good birth and education. She was motherless, having only a father and brother in Paris, and a sister away in Africa, she said. She was a kind of friendly companion in a family whose estate joined with mine; but they were liberal people and treated her as one of themselves. In a word I was at first captivated, then entangled, and finally I married. After a time we went to

Paris, where Julia was born, and there I saw her father and brother. The father was a well-mannered handsome man, with a dash of East Indian blood in him—a man for whom I had instinctively a profound horror and disgust; the son was of the same stamp, more subtle perhaps and less animal. You have seen him here, Aura."

"Mr. Dysart?"

"Yes, Gregory Field, really; my wife's name was Field; and Dysart is only assumed as a disguise. Fortunately the father died soon after my arrival, so that there was one rogue the less in the group; which was some cause for thankfulness in the desperate drama of iniquity playing round me. I do not think that she was naturally bad; I have never thought so. Inconsequent and good-natured—terrified lest I should detect the truth and know how grossly she had deceived me—dominated by her brother who made her his tool, and fond both of him and her sister, but not loving me; more afraid of me than loving—by no means a tender mother—vain, untruthful, and weak, which is often worse than wicked—she was all that a girl brought up in so evil a school would naturally become; but she was not intrinsically vicious. I have never thought that! At the best though she was bad enough for my wife, —bad enough for the name of Carthew! I am not a close-handed man, as you know, Aura, ; and having then more than my present fortune, I was well able to be generous to a young creature whom I did not love, and to whom I was glad to make amends for the want of that love, by giving her what she prized more, the free run of my purse. Yet though liberal to her, and not looking too closely into her actions, I could not be blind to the fact that she was extravagant, and got through an immense amount of money; though I saw but little show for what she spent. Large sums went; but to what result? She used to explain to me, in her coaxing childish way, that this trinket and that trifle had cost fabulous sums, when I questioned her; but I gradually became aware that she was hiding from me a deeper source of expenditure than a little lace and jewellery; though by no questioning, grave, severe, affec-

tionate, or playful, could I obtain the smallest clue
as to what it was. This determined silence, and the
cleverness with which she parried my questions
and sought to throw me on a wrong scent,
disturbed me not a little in one so inconsequent.
Had she been a resolute character throughout, I
should have understood it; but so much self-
command cropping out for only one occasion in a woman so little given to self-
command convinced me that something was
gravely wrong, and that some one outside the
house had her in full possession. It could only
be her brother; he was the sole intimate she had.
But his income was good, he lived in good style,
and never wanted money; he had inherited from
his father, he said, and I saw no reason to doubt
him. Still, much about him struck me disagree-
ably. His friends were all of a loose and dissolute
sort; I knew that he gambled; and I never heard
of his visiting at any respectable house, French or
English. Certainly, I never met him anywhere.
Once or twice too, unpleasant things happened to
myself which staggered me, and made me feel

like a man in a dream not sure of anything about him ; things for which I could not account, seeing that I had never interfered in politics, and therefore could not have put myself in false relations with the law, or subjected myself to police suspicion. My life went on in this manner for about a year, when suddenly and by chance, I one day discovered that my wife had been robbing me almost from the first day of our marriage. She had forged drafts on my banker—for unfortunately she was an adept at imitating handwriting —they all could do that most wonderfully; she had never paid a tradesman's bill, save those she was obliged to pay under fear of discovery ; and what money I had given her, had for the most part passed over to her father or brother. When I was on the verge of ruin the secret came out. Had things gone on for much longer as they were now, I should have been ruined. As it was I was crippled, and obliged to lessen my income by many hundreds, to redeem my name from the dishonour of debt. It was just before the birth of Mabel that this discovery was made ; the day before, I

think, so that I could not treat the matter with
fitting severity, nor remove her from Paris, as I
otherwise should have done, on the instant. Her
confinement gave me time however to examine
strictly into my affairs, while it kept her out of
both danger and mischief; and of course my first
act was to forbid her brother the house, and insist
on no kind of communication between him and us.
Just then the sister returned from Algeria—so
they said—where she had been acting as governess
to the only daughter of some officer of high rank,
and I trusted that her better influence would
counteract the brother's evil power, and help to
keep my wife honest and truthful for the future.
I did not know then that she was as bad as the
rest; indeed the worst of all, because the best
actress, and the most unscrupulous.

I designed, so soon as the child and mother
could bear the journey, to come to England where
I would separate her from her brother effectually,
and keep her under such surveillance that she
could not deceive me as she had done; and so I
made up my mind to bear the dishonour and

shame that I knew of in the best way I could. For my wife to have committed forgery, though only against me her husband, was a bitter humiliation to a man so proud as I and so sensitive in all that relates to honour. Still, it was unknown to any save ourselves, and I could have borne it in silence and with a wolfish kind of patience, had there been nothing more behind.

She had been for one drive only, I think, after the birth of the child, when one day on returning home I found that she had gone out, no one knew where; in fact she was missing—a clandestine sortie unexplained and unaccountable. I waited for her for some hours; and then seriously alarmed, and feeling sure that something terrible had happened, I prepared to seek her—I scarcely knew where. As I was descending the stairs, a note was given to me demanding my immediate attendance at the police office, where I found my wife—in custody for detected shop-lifting. Let me end at once," he continued in extreme agitation, "for it makes me feel as if going mad when I remember the horror of that day, and know it is all an eternal unalterable fact. I had married into a family of known and convicted swindlers, notorious throughout Paris. The mother had been an adventuress, and father and brother had been imprisoned several times for various acts of escroquerie; while the sister, just returned from Africa, had in reality been just released from prison. And now my wife who had hitherto escaped, urged by brother and sister to find them money as before, consented to become a public thief for their pleasure; but detected in slipping a diamong ring into her pocket, was henceforth and for ever inscribed on the police-books of Paris as Voleuse. There stands my name, wife, rendered infamous for ever! Now you know why I have renounced it, and why I would not suffer you or the children to bear it; why I have never told you the history of my life, and why I wished you to live and die in ignorance of it. Had the stain on my name been due to any fault or crime of my own, I would have confessed all before I had even asked you for your love; but it seemed to me better to leave it in oblivion. I was no longer

Carthew, and therefore you were not besmirched by even the shadow of the past evil. There was no landed property to leave save Croft which is not entailed, and which I could leave to our boy under any name I chose; and altogether silence seemed the better course, and would have been, had not an unlucky chance brought that scoundrel Field across my path; a mere chance surely, for no one knew what had become of me. I sold my estate, changed my bankers, dropped my name; it seemed to me that I had not left the faintest spoor by which I might be tracked; and yet—overtaken at last!"

He pressed her hand over his eyes as he said this, and Aura felt him trembling like a child. She put her arms round his neck and kissed him, perhaps with more tenderness and respect than she had ever felt before; and he knew and recognized her spirit. He knew too, that his past sorrow was conquering her present grief, and that in her sympathy with him she would lose something of the keenness of her own anguish. It is not trading on affection to understand its influence.

"You must finish the whole story now, Jasper," then said Aura gently. "One pain is better than two, and sad as it is for you—and I do feel for you, my husband"—how they clung to those precious words now! "it is better told to the end at once. How then did you think she died?"

"When she was sentenced and imprisoned," he said shuddering; "I left Paris with the children, and went to live at St. Valéry until the time of her sentence should have expired; though uncertain enough what to do with her when her term was out; and while there, I received a notification from her brother (through my banker) that she was dead. Her health had failed in prison he said, and her sentence had been respited; the brother and sister took her for change of air to Madeira, and there he said she died. It was culpably negligent in me perhaps that I did not verify the fact; but you can understand how I wished to obliterate the past, and how I dreaded any recurrence of the connection between the family and myself. Then it was that I formed my plan of concealment. I left St. Valéry; came over to

England; by chance saw the advertisement of this house; and came down here as Mr. Trelawney. You know the rest; you know everything now, my Aura, except the particulars of my two interviews with Gregory Field. When he found me here, he had me in his power. He knew by my change of name that I had parted with the past; and of course he knew that for the sake of yourself, and *her* children, I would not wish that fatal past to become known. He said that he was poor, and I could see that though flashy he was not in funds; and then he hinted at *her* being still alive. And I, who had not verified her death, who had never dreamed of its being necessary until then, was betrayed into a moment's look of terror. He saw this, and knew his power. Then he offered himself to be bought off. Like a fool I gave him money; and established him as a raw henceforth. One false step led to another. He wrote to me, asking for an interview at his lodgings, else he would force one here. I was in his power as I say, and I went—as you know. Then he distinctly told me that she was alive, and that they had made her dead to me for the furtherance of some vile plot or other then on hand. He said that she was married, but in poor circumstances; and he demanded a settlement on him for life, as the price of his silence and to keep her quiet. Again I yielded; not to the full extent, but giving him a handsome sum for the moment; and the result has been, his settling himself as a grand gentleman here at Lea Cottage, and now this frightful apparition. It may all be a plot you know, my Aura, and this woman may be the sister, or indeed any other poor wretch taught her part and hired to act it——"

"But the handwriting?" interrupted Aura.

He blenched.

"I forgot that," he said, and bent his head gloomily.

"But you said that they all could imitate handwritings well; are you *sure* this is hers?"

"It is more than ten years since I saw hers," he answered; "and it may have changed a little. This is singularly like hers, but still it may be the sister's imitation."

"Can you do nothing to find out the truth?"

cried Aura. "Anything would be better than this suspense!"

"Now; but suspense was better than the truth, if the truth would have been destruction," said Jasper in a low voice. "I was afraid of the truth, Aura, but I would brave it now, with this hand in mine."

"Did you write to Madeira?" asked Aura; "since that man came here, I mean. Have you made any inquiries of the consul there, or of the English clergyman? Funchal is not a large place; such a thing as a death would not be difficult to verify, even if so long ago as ten years."

"I have not written," he replied; "I was afraid."

"Fear will not help us through," returned Aura; "we must face our danger and understand our position; we must grasp our nettle, Jasper, and know the truth, no matter what the pain and sacrifice."

"Certainly, my wife; our position, or rather mine, is altered now, and I would search out the reality of this horror as steadily as yourself. I will write by the next post to the consul at

Funchal, and to the English clergyman; we shall hear something in reply."

"May I counsel you, Jasper?—you so much wiser than I!"

"May you—may you love me, my Aura?" he answered fondly.

"You can trust me?"

"Yes, as my own soul; both for strength and courage."

"Well then, you must go to Madeira and see into this for yourself," she said.

"And leave you here alone in this nest of hornets, Aura?" cried Jasper in dismay.

"Guarding your name, your love, and your children till your return," she answered with a melancholy smile, tears filling her eyes. "You may trust me. However sharp their stings, they shall not drive me from my post. Take my advice, Jasper! there is nothing to hide from me now, and we shall be able to act so much better when we know all—even the worst. But can you see this person who has written?" she exclaimed suddenly, as a new thought struck her. "Can you meet her here, or even force yourself into her presence, though she says, does she not, that she will not see you? That looks as if she was afraid to face you, Jasper, does it not?" she added eagerly; and then, in an altered voice, "or it may mean simply what she says, that she is generous? Oh, my Jasper, to think that I should hold you by the generosity of any woman!" she cried clinging to him, half in love and half in shame.

"You hold me, and are held by me, by Love," said Jasper; "and that no one can disturb."

"Will you go down to the village now and see her?" then said Aura, feverishly impatient and restless to know the truth the soonest possible. "You can easily find where she is lodging; and if you were to see her, that might end all at once, and spare you the long journey to Madeira, and save me from the long, long weary absence."

"And if——" he hesitated.

"You must not let her want," she said, lifting her eyes to his. "She has been your wife; she is the mother of your children; and she must not be left to misery, however weak or wicked in her career."

"I was not thinking of her," said Jasper, bending his face to Aura's. "I was thinking of you."

"I cannot decide yet," she said, turning herself half away, while with one hand she held his to her bosom and laid the other on his shoulder. "So many feelings! so many opposing duties! Give me time, but give me certainty first, my Jasper. Till we have this certainty you are mine and I am yours. Let us wait until we know for the rest."

"You could not leave me, Aura?"

"Could I stay?" she said quivering. "You would not be my husband then!"

"I am your husband, Aura, and you are my wife in the sight of God; whatever the legal flaw. To abandon me would be to abandon your husband for the world — the truth for a show."

"I have the children to think of also," she

answered hurriedly. "The wrong—if there has been any wrong done to them—was done innocently until now; but what would it be in the eyes of the world if I continued in it when I knew the truth?"

"Still the world!" said Jasper sighing.

He forgot that it was his own dread of this very world he was now contemning, which had placed them in their present fatal circumstances, and that if he could have braved a few days' scornful gossip he would not have needed now to ask for love instead of fear.

"Let it rest till we know," said Aura; "let our love and our hope be enough for the present. I will not leave you, Jasper, my beloved! unless God speaks to my soul and bids me!"

"Then you will not leave me at all," said Jasper hastily; "for Eternal Truth will not bid you sacrifice the truth to social form, and Love will not bid you sacrifice love for the poor mockery of the world's approval! Be guided by the voice of truth and love, Aura, which means the voice of God, and I shall fear nothing; but that is not the voice which will speak to you from Clive Vale. Now I must be going, my wife. I shall soon be back again, but every moment away from you now seems an eternity."

He kissed her tenderly, she trembling rather than weeping, but he nerved now with the strength which comes to men when in action, however dangerous or terrible in its chances. It is the dead weight of inaction that kills a man; the passive waiting on events, and non-resistance under wrong : and Jasper, now that he might act, was all his old strong sinewy self again, and neither wept nor trembled, neither feared nor faltered.

His visit to the village was in vain. "Madame Shanter had gone away that afternoon," said Mrs. Makemson, at whose house he soon heard that she was lodging; "and would not be back again, so far as she knew. Any letters that might come for her were to be left till called for, but she did not say who would call for them or when. At all events she had gone and taken her portmantel with her, and no one knew nothing more."

So Jasper returned to his sad home, no nearer advanced than before; and the next day he set out on his strange journey to Madeira. And now Aura was left alone to bear the bursting of the storm as she best might: their first separation for six years; and the occasion of it to determine whether she was his lawful wife or no, and if her children had a right to their father's name!

CHAPTER IX.

———◦◦◦———

WHEN Jasper went, " Madame de Chantreau "
came back. That mysterious little bird which
goes about whispering to people who had better
remain deaf, told the Parisian adventuress that
the coast was clear, so she might set sail and go win
what wealth and laurels she could. In obedience
to which intelligence she hastened to return to
cette bonne Madame Makéson, as she called her ;
and, acting on a telegram from London which
seemed to relate only to a cap and a bonnet, prepared to lay siege to Aura, or rather to Aura's
purse ; adding to this larger outline independent
sketches of any gain or amusement that might
be practicable.

Fear formed a large portion of Madame Louise

Trébuchet's life, and she counted on it in her dealings with others. Now too that Jasper was away she was not afraid of a recognition, which under all the circumstances might be a little awkward and premature; so she prepared to roam about the Vale at her ease, dressed with even greater care and her face made up with more wonderful artistry, not unwilling to put herself in the way of others besides les petites, if so be that others were available.

By this time however, every one was as anxious to see her as she was to see them; for the news had flown through the Vale that the foreign lady at Mrs. Makemson's had met Mr. Trelawney's two little French girls, and had kissed and "carried on" over them; so of course, who could she be but their mother? — the only mystery remaining being—was she married or unmarried? The Vale had not quite made up its mind on which count to condemn Mr. Trelawney, but he was to be condemned on one.

"Pardon, monsieur, je suis étrangère; I am a stranger in your land," said a clear flutelike voice in Mr. Bennet's ear, as he was walking moodily along the road, thinking of no one else but that identical little Frenchwoman stealing so swiftly and so noiselessly behind him; building up a day-dream, if the truth must be told, of how that she was a decided Roman Catholic (as he made no doubt she was) but with such plastic faith that he could mould her into the likeness of the severest Calvinism he knew of, and so receive her publicly into the true Church, as his own special work. The glory of one undeniable conversion would have made Mr. Bennet for life; Romanism and all its avenues, and atheism and all its avenues, dividing the Pit between them in his mind. At the sound of that birdlike voice he turned sharply round, the unexpected answer to his thoughts startling him; and taking off his hat made his most pompous clerical bow, which crisped madame's rosy lips with laughter hard to be subdued.

"I would ask of your goodness, monsieur, to direct me to a certain wood which gives on to a marais," she said with enchanting simplicity, folding her hands together; she wore the most perfectly fitting pale lavender gloves, and Mr. Bennet thought himself a connoisseur in hands and feet.

"Do you mean Lea Woods, madam?" he asked.

"Précisement!" she cried smiling. "It is Lea Woods that I would indicate. Can monsieur show me the route? A relative of my hostess lives there sick, and I would carry her a little soulagement—if not held to be impertinente."

Mr. Bennet's face lightened up. Not that he particularly cared for material soulagements to the poor, sick or well, but because this readiness to visit them gave him hopes of the future. But what if she should be a Popish emissary, with the whole creed and craft of Jesuitism in her pocket? Willing as he was to accept the little lady, it behoved him to keep his eyes open, and to remember the text relating to wolves in sheep's clothing.

"I am going that way myself," he said, "and perhaps to the same person, Tabitha Hodson?

and if you are not afraid of being in company with
a Protestant minister, I shall be very happy to
accompany you."

"Merci, monsieur," she said, bending her head
graciously and gracefully; "why afraid? Au
contraire, the character of prêtre is one sacred to
me." Here she raised her eyes sweetly.

"But you are a Roman Catholic?" asked
Mr. Bennet.

She gave a little scream—

"L'horreur!" she said. "No, monsieur, not
the least au monde. I am a Protestant pure and
simple—Luthérane jusqu'aux ongles. I to have
dealings with all these superstitions, these masses
and saints and priests and confessions! I despise
them all.—I must do penance for this," she said
to herself; but Madame Louise could face even
the saints when she had an object in view.

Mr. Bennet held out his hand—

"I am glad of it, madam," he said, and shook
her hand heartily; though his day-dream about
the public reception of a converted Papist faded
into thin air, and his grand clerical castle in Spain

tumbled into ruins as she spoke. "But why then," somewhat waggishly, tempering his sacerdotal rebuke with a dash of gallantry, "why have I not seen you at church, one of the lambs of my flock? You have been here over one Sunday, I think; why did we not see you in God's house bearing your witness for the precious truth?"

"I was so unfortunate, monsieur!" said Madame Louise meekly, throwing into her reply the air of a chidden child receiving its correction penitently; "une affreuse migraine, a frightful headache, held me to my bed, so that unfortunately for me I could not go to join in your beautiful service, greatly to my affliction I assure you."

Her brother had forbidden her to go, as we know. He was afraid of the likeness between them.

"But next Sunday I shall have the pleasure of seeing you there?"

She bowed.

"Truly," she said, "I have the full intention."

"You have been long abroad, I suppose?" continued Mr. Bonnet; "but I presume that you are English?"

"Oh yes, indeed I am," cried Madame Louise clasping her hands.

"And how does England seem to you now that you have come back to it?" said Mr. Bennet; "do you like it, or is it always dull and grave?"

"Oh, monsieur, the joy to me of revisiting my native land—the fields, the trees, the tongue, the people!—none but the poor exile comprehends the exquise delight of all this."

"I am very glad," said Mr. Bennet with a brightened face; "that shows that foreign life has not spoilt you."

She cast down her eyes, but made a graceful little curtsey, looking much pleased. She was so simple and unaffected — such a little thing pleased her!—and so modest that the not very burning praise of the saturnine curate seemed almost to oppress her.

"I have sought to hold myself becomingly to my faith and nation," she answered in a low voice; and Mr. Bennet thought he had never seen a little woman more becoming both, or more after his own ideal.

"You are lodging at Mrs. Makemson's?" he continued. "Do you find her a comfortable kind of person now to deal with?"

"Oh yes; she is très bonne femme, truly admirable for me," answered the lady.

"And do you not know the Trelawneys, too?" he asked. He had heard a rumour of the meeting with the children, and what he had heard made him wish for more.

"The Trelawneys?" she answered wonderingly. "No; the Carthews I knew—pas ces autres. Oh, pardon my unfortunate tongue!" she cried covered with confusion. It is so difficult for me to feign, monsieur! Yes, yes, the Trelawneys; yes, I know the elder children a little."

But Mr. Bennet was too sharp for her. Or rather, he was just as sharp as she wished him to be—no more.

"You said another name, madam," he cried, stopping in the middle of the road and looking at her fixedly; "you know Mr. Trelawney by another name, it seems; is he really then this—— what? this Mr. Carthew, as you said?"

"Ah, what can I say!" exclaimed Madame Louise greatly distressed. "To me to lie, c'est impossible. Oui, monsieur, I have known him by that other name, and by no other. This Monsieur Trelawney is veritably Monsieur Carthew. He has abandoned his true name since he deserted me."

"Good heavens!" ejaculated Mr. Bennet flushing up; "then the man is a villain after all! —I always thought so."

"Ah, I am grieved, I am distressed!" said the lady almost tearfully, clasping her small hands round her companion's arm. For when people are in earnest and strongly moved, you know, the conventionalities and artificial reserves of society go to the wall. "It was such a mis-hazard. I am so irritated against myself that I was assez bête to speak without reflection. It may not be, monsieur, that Monsieur Carthew is all bad; there is no person who is all bad—no; and even mon pauvre Jaspaire—Monsieur Carthew I would say "—recovering herself with touching dignity, "has his beautiful side."

"He!" exclaimed Mr. Bennet fiercely, "has

the devil a beautiful side! He is a man of sin,
madam, corrupt and given up to wickedness."

"We women forgive," said Madame Louise
with a patient smile, unclasping her hands to
press a fine worked scented handkerchief delicately
to her eyes.

"Why do you cry?" asked Mr. Bennet.

"I have cause," answered Louise sighing.

"What cause? Forgive me if I seem blunt and
peremptory; but this man's condition, and the
truth about him, are of great moment to us all
here, as you can understand; and of course your
coming here set the whole place in a flame and
stirred up all the old reports: which is only natural
you must admit."

"I am so sorry!" said the lady. "I came but
to see my children—my two dearest little girls.
I wanted to see them en cachette—secretly, you
know, so as not to waken suspicion, or disturb the
peace of this poor dame that I cannot en vouloir,
though she has done me so much wrong. I have
seen them, and criminally weak I cannot tear
myself away from the sacred spot that contains

them. I am haunted by their dear little visages, monsieur," and she wept touchingly : " it seems to me so cruel that I may not see them daily !—I who have held them to my heart new-born ! Ah, monsieur, you gentlemen cannot understand these weaknesses of the poor woman's heart ! "

" I am sorry for you, madam," said Mr. Bennet ; " and sorry too for her, the poor, misguided obdurate woman ! " but his sorrow was warmth for Madame Louise, and bitterness for Aura : " and what I can do to obtain you justice and redress, I will. I may be able to do more for you than you think for perhaps."

" Merci, monsieur ! you are too good for me ! " the little woman answered gratefully. " Surely too is she, cette pauvre dame, to be pitied. She holds herself both better and worse than me. She has all the better semblances, and some material advantages as well—the children, money, station, his love !———"

" His love ! " sneered Mr. Bennet ; " I would give it a harsher name ! "

" ———While I am poor, deprived of all, even my

nom de mariée," continued Louise, not noticing the interruption. "When he slipped me with the children, and left me to fight alone the world, and when I heard of his marriage—which I heard of too late to prevent, unhappily—then I effaced myself and took the name of de Chantreau, which is mine by right of my mother, who was a de Chantreau: a very noble family with us, monsieur," she added parenthetically. "Instinct called too hard to be unobeyed; and I came to see the children I had loved in their cradles. I laid too heavy a weight on my heart, and failed to hold myself concealed, as you may have heard, monsieur; love such as mine is hard to beat down! and now I must fly; and again retire into the depths of this cold world, unknown and unloved by what is dearest to me in life!"

She raised her eyes and hands to heaven, and her lips moved. Mr. Bennet took it to be a prayer that she was repeating: she was not even mumbling a charm.

"No," said the curate sternly, "you must not go, madam; the thing must be brought to an

issue, and Mrs. Trelawney must be made to understand her position, and all its fatal guilt. Living
with a married man as his wife—a case of bigamy
that he could be prosecuted for, not to speak of
the intense sinfulness of the whole matter—no,
madam! such a scandal shall not be permitted to
continue in my parish!"

"Oh, no! no!" she interrupted him with a
piteous accent. "My poor Jaspaire! I could not
harm him, monsieur! Indeed no! my only course
is to retire now speedily, and leave them to their
happiness in peace."

"And leave her in her sin?" asked Mr. Bennet
severely.

She cast down her eyes.

"That goes with her own conscience," she said.

"But she must and shall know her true state,"
said Mr. Bennet impetuously.

"She does," answered Madame Louise slowly.

"She does? and has not left him?"

She shook her head.

"Then she shall," said Mr. Bennet in a low
voice, "if I stir heaven and earth for it!"

"Monsieur is a righteous man," said Madame Louise. And Mr. Bennet felt that he was.

Then they continued their walk to Lea Woods, where they visited Tabitha Hodson together; how poor old Tabitha stared at the Parisian vision in its silks and satins, which brought the odour of Guerlain's so strongly into the little cottage that the sick woman said she must dee outright if they could not get rid of it for her!—and when there, Madame Louise slipped her purse into Mr. Bennet's hand, saying in a low voice : "Permit me to make you my almoner." Which, as Mr. Bennet said afterwards, was the handsomest thing he had ever known of any one, and what all persons with a proper respect for the cloth should do, when they wished to give alms. Such as it was, it was the cleverest thing the clever little woman had done yet; and if the conquest of Mr. Bennet had been as important as it was easy, Madame Louise Field Trébuchet de Chantreau would have come to the end of her manœuvring without much further trouble.

When they parted, which they did before they

entered the village, both with one accord shrinking
from public notice, Mr. Bennet was more deeply
smitten with the little French lady than he had
ever been in his life before, save perhaps with
Aura at the time when he made her an offer of
marriage, and tried to kiss her into consent. Not
that he acknowledged this to himself. If narrow,
harsh, and therefore essentially unchristian, he
was a man of pure morals and strict integrity,
and would not have permitted any laxity to himself
that he would have denounced in another. He liked
to hold a large spiritual harem where he was the
central divinity—the Vishnù filling all hearts—
but this was all; and his flirtations as yet had
never descended into personalities; but Madame
de Chantreau——. Perhaps it was his new-born
if unacknowledged feeling for her that barbed the
shaft he longed to fling into Croft, and which he
intended to fling too—with an aim that could not
miss—and braced his soul into Rhadamanthine
likeness, owning no pity and feeling no ruth.
Mr. Bennet was of the stuff of which inquisitors
are made. He might have been of Alva's crew,

or Claverhouse's; but he was no Tartuffe: which made him all the more bitter enemy where he was an enemy at all.

After then he had left Madame Louise at the entrance of the village—before the entrance indeed —he went straight up to the Rectory; and there struck Mr. and Mrs. Escott to the ground with the terror of his news. There was no getting over it — there was no explaining it away—no excusing—no retaliating. Here was a lady who openly proclaimed herself the wife of Mr. Jasper Trelawney and the mother of his children, and who also added the startling fact that he was not Mr. Jasper Trelawney at all, but a Mr. Carthew; thus adding lie upon lie, and sin upon sin. Already married—the deserter of his wife—and living here under a false name—could they allow their daughter to remain another day in that house of sin? that temple of Belial, as he, Mr. Bennet, had always known it to be? He had been put down harshly, and his word had not been taken; yet, if his keener spiritual perceptions had been believed in, what a tragedy and what guilt might not have been spared!

But when he entered on his self-glorification, the poor old Rector, who hitherto had sat with his face buried in his hands like one stricken with death, unable to reply to words however cruel yet seemingly only too true, suddenly lifted up his head and told the curate fiercely to mind his own business, which was quite as much as he could do to do well; and to find the front door as soon as he conveniently could. He had always been disagreeable to him as he well knew, but now he was hateful; and he bade him out of his sight at once. Who was he indeed, to come and gloat over an old man's miseries? and how did he, Mr. Escott, know what of all this cock-and-bull story was true, and what Mr. Bennet had made up himself? With other of the wounded man's wild blows, hitting right and left in the air, blinded with his own blood. The interview ended stormily, as might be expected; and Mr. Bennet left the Rectory in most unrighteous anger, telling Mr. Escott that the ruin which had fallen on his house

was a judgment on his pride and obstinacy and
want of spiritual truth, and that he saw the hand
of God in it all, smiting him to the earth through
his children for his sins, as Eli the High Priest
was smitten in olden time. Had the two men
been anything but "of the cloth," there would
have been blows at the Rectory that day before
Mr. Bennet finally withdrew.

By the evening the whole Vale was in an
uproar, blazing with the fiery words that Mr.
Trelawney was a scoundrel, and not Mr. Trelawney
at all; that Aura was not his wife, but only a poor
castaway; and that "the strange lady at Makemson's there, had the right to be at Croft, if right
got its due." And sorry as they all were for
Aura—and they were sorry for her, for was she
not one of their own?—there was scarcely one in
all the Vale that would have missed the news
which stirred up its blood as it liked to have
it stirred, with a first-class sensation not to be
explained away as "idle gossip not worth repeating
or believing." Only the more charitable hoped
that something would turn up, they knew not

what or how, by which things would come right again after they had been put wrong. In which the Vale was not singular, either in its relish for a "row," or its belief in the social miracle of rehabilitation.

CHAPTER X.

It was a strange kind of instinct that took most of the Valcites to the Hollics the next day. And yet it was natural. They could not go to their old meeting-place the Rectory, to discuss the momentous business then on hand; for small as was the delicacy among them, even they understood that it was scarcely a matter on which they could speak in grand committee with the Escotts. One or two singly might indeed approach it tenderly, but not a whole party of them together—not such a gathering as filled the Hollics' drawing-room, and made it look like a country " At home." They all came much about the same time too; which gave more importance to the meeting, and prevented wasteful repetitions.

And among the rest bustled in Mr. Grainger terribly agitated and distressed. Now that the thing had really come upon them, and he met " Miss Aura's " ruin face to face, he wished that it had not been stirred at all, and that this woman had broken her neck before ever she came to the Vale to destroy that poor lady's life. And yet—he was a religious man, and felt keenly the sin of her condition if consciously continued in and if absolutely true. And where was it all to stop ? Bigamy was a prosecutable offence—what if there was a trial and a conviction, and Mr. Trelawney sentenced to imprisonment ? Such degradation for the poor dear girl he had known so long and had always liked through everything, and who had carried herself so high ! As Mr. Grainger walked to the Hollies this morning, he more than once surprised a vagrant tear stealing down his prim leathery face as he pictured the ruined future and the broken heart of beautiful Aura Trelawney. He had a queer temper as his neighbours said ; he was stiff and prudish and gossipy and small-minded, and ill-natured too, but he was a kind-hearted man at bottom, though more than once he had a vision of calling Mr. Trelawney out and shooting him through the heart for his treachery. The visions of a man deeply stirred are no fit measure of his ordinary temper. Patrick Grainger was as capable of heading an insurrection against the Queen as of calling out any one; or of shooting him if he did.

"I am glad to meet so many of our friends here to-day, Mrs. Price," began Mr. Bennet, taking up the theme at once; "for I think it necessary that some definite line of action should be taken in the terrible affair now agitating all minds; and a concerted line—the Vale acting as one person—so that we may have no unhappy party spirit or social divisions, but may all understand distinctly what is our righteous course, and what we are bound to do."

"I do not think, Mr. Bennet, you know much about the matter," said Mr. Grainger irritably; "and you had better have left it to those who do."

"The question is a public one, Mr. Grainger,

on which we can all judge equally," retorted Mr. Bennet; "and from my standing and profession alone, if for no other more special qualifications, I consider myself the fittest person to open the discussion."

"Your standing and profession, sir, may be all very fine," said Mr. Grainger bristling up; "but you are comparatively a stranger here; you have no enduring tie among us."

"Mr. Grainger, have you seen the lady and conversed with her yourself?" said Mr. Bennet excitedly; "for if you have not, I have."

"You have seen this foreign lady, Mr. Bennet?" cried Mrs. Price; and all eyes turned upon him much as if he had said he had seen the sea serpent or the dodo.

"Yes; I have had a long conversation with her, and found her a most estimable person, with a deep sense of religion, a firm Protestant, and altogether a most charming and delightful lady."

"And who is she then?" asked Mrs. Price.

Amid the dead silence of the room Mr. Bennet

said slowly, but in a high-pitched and distinct voice—

"The mother of the elder two young ladies, and Mr. Trelawney's wife."

"I don't believe it," shouted Mr. Grainger. "I'll bet five pounds she is an adventuress!"

But he shouted in vain, and no one heeded him.

Then Mr. Bennet told the story of his conversation with Madame de Chantreau, and all that was said on either side; and when he had ended, it was about as much like the truth as the last version of the anecdote in "Russian scandal" is like the first. He did not mean to be untruthful, but he came to the same result. For all at which Madame Louise had only hinted he detailed in round terms; and all that she had barely indicated he formularized in broad unmistakable lines; and what she had merely insinuated he told as positive and proven; and so, mere unsubstantial shadows came to be flesh-and-blood realities, and the Vale had nothing left for it but to believe its spokesman, and to follow the path hewn out by its pioneer. There was no doubt of it in the minds of any there, save perhaps Mr. Grainger; and he was mainly actuated by jealousy of Mr. Bennet and the instinct of opposition; but with all the rest the thing was settled— Madame de Chantreau was the true Mrs. Trelawney, or rather she was Mrs. Carthew—they hardly knew how to call the Master of Croft now; and Aura was a poor ruined creature, as yet innocent though degraded. It rested only with herself whether she would be guilty and degraded.

"It is a mercy that Mr. Trelawney, or Carthew, or whatever the man's name is, has left Croft, as I understand he has — of course not daring to face this unhappy wife. of his," said Mrs. Price sternly. "We may do something more with that unfortunate young woman, now that his influence is withdrawn. But indeed, I doubt if any of us will do much. I know her so well, and the hopeless obduracy of her disposition! I should not in the least wonder if she went on living with him, and brazened it out. It is like her."

"She cannot, Mrs. Price! she cannot!" cried

Mr. Bennet. "If she does, she must leave the place; if not, it might cost the Rector his living."

Which would not be the worst thing that could happen at Clive Vale, in Mr. Bennet's estimation; as then he should apply for it, and he made no doubt—self-satisfied people never do doubt—that the bishop would give it to him.

"Poor thing!" said Miss Campbell compassionately; "what a dreadful position to be in!"

"Then she should not have married him at the first," sniffed Miss Mason, settling her bonnet strings; "and if she had taken the advice of older and wiser people she would never have got herself into this mess."

"I wonder if there will be a prosecution for bigamy?" suggested Mrs. Mountain, with rather more animation than usual. "Mountain had a very great case once in his hands, but then it was the husband who turned up again after they had thought him lost in the bush in Australia. He managed it very well, the judge said, and I believe got complimented in full court. It was in the papers they said, but I did not see it for myself."

"Some one ought to write to the brother," said Major Morgan. "As an old Indian officer myself, I should perhaps be able to soften the blow to him better than any one else would."

"The Rector will do that, I should suppose," returned Mrs. Price.

"Ah!" cried Mr. Grainger spitefully, "if young Mr. Herbert comes home, some one had better look out! for if all this is a much-ado-about-nothing sort of a business, as I have my shrewd suspicions it will turn out to be, some one will get kicked through the place, I'll lay any money of it; and perhaps it will not be Mr. Trelawney!" looking full at Mr. Bennet as he spoke.

"Oh! Mr. Grainger, you are always so fierce!" remonstrated Mrs. Price, "I am sure no one has said harder things of this man than you have; and I must say it seems very odd that you should turn round now and be his advocate."

"And I think it much more odd, Mrs. Price, that all of you should take the opinion of such a

man as Mr. Bennet, who, without meaning anything unpleasant to him but just the contrary,
cannot be a very good judge of strange women
French or English, and rush off at once to the
belief that this person coming from the clouds is
Mr. Trelawney's wife because she says so. If I
now, or Major Morgan," a little contemptuously,
" or Mr. Dysart, or any man accustomed to the
world and used to deal with all sorts of people—
were to see and question this woman, that would
be a different thing ; but till I have better authority than our curate's, I must beg to keep out of
the plot altogether, and to regard Mrs. Trelawney
as Mrs. Trelawney until she is proved not so."

"Oh ! we all know the weakness *there*," said
Mrs. Price satirically.

" Your determination is in accordance with your
character, sir," sneered Mr. Bennet. " You have
never been on the right side in anything, and never
will, until you are converted and a heart of grace
is given you in place of your present impenitent
heart of sin."

" Go to the devil, you impudent coxcomb !"

muttered Patrick Grainger taking his hat. "Ladies, I wish you all good-morning," he said, bowing with extraordinary stiffness; "and if Mr. Trelawney indites certain members of our society for a conspiracy, it will be only what they deserve and what I hope they will get." Saying which he left the room, determined to find this foreign lady and judge for himself what she was worth.

Soon after this the meeting broke up, with the resolution, assented to in an informal, of course, kind of way, that if Aura persisted in remaining at Croft when she knew her true position, she must be "cut," and representation of the case made to the bishop. The last was Mr. Bennet's rider; but adopted as a mysterious kind of appeal entailing penalties of gigantic proportions, if shadowy. And that they might be sure she did know her position— and that without any false delicacy or weak mincing of truth, and calling a spade by any other name than a spade—Mrs. Price announced her intention of going up to Croft herself. If she could prevail on Mr. and Mrs. Escott to accompany her, so much the better; but accompanied or not she

would go up now at once to Croft, and there detail
to Aura the truth and her duty.

"La! poor Mrs. Trelawney!" said Miss Campbell shuddering; "I should not like to be in her
place this afternoon!"

"My dear, I would rather face a burglar than
Mrs. Price in a preaching fit," returned Miss
Mason. And then they both shook hands with
her cordially, and said she was quite right to do
her duty so steadfastly. People are such hypo-
crites to bony women of strong tempers and the
habit of speaking their minds!

Mrs. Price found the poor old Rector and his
wife on the point of starting for Croft; and it was
not very difficult even for her to understand that
she was a nuisance to them, and they would rather
be without her. But she was of the class not
tender-hearted as to whose toes it treads on and
whose shoulders it rubs; and as she came there
meaning to fasten herself on to them, she fastened
herself accordingly, and took no heed of the incon-
venience caused by her presence. Indeed she
rather liked to annoy people than not, having always

some object in view which made her lawfully disagreeable, and holding pain and discomfort to be the best regimen humanity could be put under. So they went up to Croft together, and found, as they expected, that Aura was at home. Mrs. Escott asked for "my daughter;" with Mrs. Price's eyes upon her she would not have dared to ask for "Mrs. Trelawney."

Aura was in the drawing-room surrounded by the children. Tiny was sitting gravely by her side on the sofa, with her favourite doll like a battered old Feejee idol in her lap, learning to sew with a blunt needle on a bit of pink flannel; Dotty was making herself happy over a coloured pencil and a white slate, and drawing what he said were fairies, but what looked like caterpillars; Julia and Mabel were sitting in the bay of the window, talking of the strange lady who had met them that day, and telling stories to each other in turn while doing some wonderful stuff they called tatting—but half the loops were wrong with Mabel's, though Julia's was well enough; and Aura had baby in her arms, crowing out his wet-lipped observations on life in general, as she held him kicking on her knee, making believe to stand, with one naked foot like a ball of rose leaves and the other in a blue shoe, as was more befitting his condition. It was such a picture of beauty and love that any one but obtuse Mrs. Escott would have felt its charm; and none but Mrs. Price could have foreseen its destruction with such grim satisfaction. To her mind it looked a little heathenish somehow, as if it was sinful and unreal. But then Mrs. Price was not what one would call a womanly woman, or as Kingsley would say a "cuddling pussy mamma;" but regarded children chiefly as immortal souls to be disciplined from the beginning, and in no wise as live dolls to be loved and played with and fondled and delighted in, irrespective of the future.

Aura rose to meet them as they came into the room, a little paler and thinner than usual, but in manner and bearing the same as ever; "hardened," said Mrs. Price, who expected to see her oppressed with shame, and unable to lift her eyes. At least she did not expect, as she said to Zillah afterwards; she only hoped against hope that it

would be so. If any change was noticeable
at all, it was that she was a shade more self-
possessed; and to Mrs. Price—divining by instinct on what errand she had come—a shade more
formal.

Mrs. Escott kissed her and began to cry. "My
poor miserable daughter!" she said; and when the
Rector kissed her, he too gave something that was
ominously like a sob, and pressed her to his heart
with unusual fervour. Mrs. Price said stiffly; "I
am glad to see you bear up so well, Aura." She
had never called her Aura before; but that evaded
the difficulty of the name, and was reassuring to
begin with, if she would behave herself properly.
And then Aura understood all that was coming,
and what she should have to battle through.

She made no answer to any of the three opening
demonstrations; but, still with baby in her arms,
rang the bell twice, and delivered the children up
to the nurses; the boy and Tiny being rapt away
in a duet of shrieks.

"Aura, you must come home with me to-day,"
said Mrs. Escott, casting the first shell into the
magazine.

"Why, dear mamma?" Aura answered. "I am afraid I cannot while my husband is away, as I promised him that I would not leave the children. You know he is always anxious about them, and I am sure that he would be very miserable in his first absence from us if he felt he could not trust me implicitly."

"You must come and bring the children with you; your own I mean; of course not the others; they have their own mother to look after them now," returned Mrs. Escott panting, and making a ball of her handkerchief.

"I know of no other mother for Julia and Mabel than myself," said Aura with emphasis.

"We do," said Mrs. Price slowly.

"Indeed?" with a stately inclination of her head.

"Do you mean to say you are ignorant of what all the Vale knows and is ringing with?" asked Mrs. Price sitting very upright.

"I am not ignorant that a strange woman is in the village, who gives herself out as my husband's wife [and the mother of my adopted children,"

answered Aura, looking her full in the face; " but
I have yet to learn that the bold assertions of a
mere adventuress are to regulate my life and destroy
my home."

" That is simple subterfuge," said Mrs. Price.
" Adventuress!—adventuresses do not come down
into country places and claim as their husbands
gentlemen living there, without some reason for it.
The thing is preposterous, when half a moment's
interview would settle the whole question—if there
could be any question of mistaken identity or false im-
personation. If this gentleman—this Mr. Carthew "
—Aura gave a visible start at this name, and Mrs.
Price saw it—" ah! I see you know that too! "
she said spitefully, " as you most probably know
everything; if then this gentleman whom we
have known by the name of Trelawney, but who
is, as you are aware, Mr. Carthew," with a cruel
dwelling on the syllables—" if he was really innocent and above suspicion, how could such a thing
have ever happened to him ? Would it be possible
for any woman in the world to come forward and
claim Mr. Escott, for instance, as her husband

before your mother ?—or if she did, would she not be taken up at once as a maniac or impostor? Instead of which, here has Mr. Trelawney—Carthew rather—run away from his lady, because, as we all know, he is afraid to face her!"

"I do not know so," said Aura quietly.

"It looks like it, my dear," said the Rector gently.

"We cannot always judge from appearances, dear papa," answered his daughter.

"Very true, my dear; no, no, we cannot," he returned, and shuffled to the window.

"There is no smoke without some fire, Aura," cried Mrs. Escott; "and unless Mr. Trelawney had behaved ill in some way or other, a nice lady-like person as this is by all accounts, could not come down and claim the children and the father in this offhanded manner. It is all very well to say adventuress and all that, but such things don't happen now-a-days as if we were all Mrs. Radcliffes and Monk Lewises."

"I know nothing, and can believe nothing, beyond what my husband tells me," said Aura.

"Husband!" sneered Mrs. Price.

"You ought to believe what your father and I tell you, Aura," fired up Mrs. Escott, "and not be always thrusting this man in our faces, as if there was no one in the world worth living for or believing in but himself."

"He is the chief to me," said Aura.

"Then it does not sound well to hear you stand up for him in this manner, all things considered," said Mrs. Escott angrily.

"I should have thought that any woman with a proper sense of dignity and self-respect even, not to speak of virtue, would have flown from such a position as yours on the very first breath of suspicion," said Mrs. Price severely. "It is really terrible to see you so lost to all womanly modesty, and to all sense of duty religious and moral."

"We read the laws of duty and morality differently," said Aura, with great quietness of manner but with great firmness. "To me it seems a woman's duty and dignity to believe in her husband, even if appearances are against him, which I do not allow they are in this case, with any one who can *trust*—to love him through good report and evil report alike—and to remain with him under all circumstances."

" Whether his wife or not ? " asked Mrs. Price.

" Under all such circumstances as these of my present position," answered Aura slowly.

" In which case I, as a lawfully married woman and the mother of virtuous daughters, have no business here," said Mrs. Price rising.

Aura bowed and rang the bell—

" I agree with you," she said haughtily, and stood waiting for the lady to go.

" I declare, Aura, you are quite indelicate in your love for that man ! " cried Mrs. Escott.

Mrs. Price smiled sourly—

" What can you expect, Mrs. Escott, from the willing mistress of a profligate ? " she said.

At that moment the servant came into the room.

" Robert," said Aura, with all and more than all Jasper's haughtiness added to her own native dignity, " open the door to Mrs. Price, and remember, if she calls again, I am not at home to her."

"You need not be alarmed, Miss Escott!" said Mrs. Price; "I am not likely to do so, not being in the habit of associating with kept mistresses as a rule. This house is no fit place for any respectable woman to be seen in, and you may be very sure it has seen me for the last time."

"Show Mrs. Price out," repeated Aura grandly.

And the house door of Croft closed against the lady of the Hollies for ever.

"How can you be so imprudent, Aura!" sobbed Mrs. Escott; "at a time when you want all the friends you can get—and all will be few enough, that I can tell you!—to go and affront her like this! You have lost your senses I think; if you ever had any to lose; but I don't think you ever had—pride and obstinacy have eaten them away long since."

"It was rashly done, my dear," said the Rector; "you have made her an enemy for life."

"What would you have had me do, dear papa? submit to her insults?"

"Stuff and nonsense, Aura! how do you know they were insults and not the truth?" cried Mrs. Escott. "If this young woman is Mr. Trelawney's wife, as she says—and how in the name of fortune can she say so if she is not, I should like to know?—why of course you are not his wife, and you are his mistress, and it's of no use calling things out of their names. And how you can bear to think of such a thing with all those blessed babies about you, I am sure I cannot tell! When I came in to-day and saw that little man crowing in your lap with his shoe off, and I thought that perhaps there was not one among them that was as it should be, my heart nearly broke, it did; and you as bold and quiet about it, sitting on the sofa as if everything was your own, and nothing was wrong. You certainly are incomprehensible to me, Aura."

"My dear! my dear! how you do run on," said the Rector deprecatingly.

"Will you let me speak to you very distinctly, mamma?" said Aura, standing before her mother with a strange mixture of tenderness and resolve upon her face.

"Distinctly, Aura! I am sure I never wanted you to mumble, as you do sometimes, as if you had peas in your mouth! The more distinctly you speak the better I shall like it, I'm sure; for I am quite deaf in one ear now with all this worry, and the other is going fast."

"What I want to say is this," resumed Aura: "if by some miracle this story should prove to be true, and the grave be found to have given up its dead—if so proved, I say, I will not stand between my husband and his first wife, if he wishes for her instead of me; but if he does not——"

"Hush! hush! my girl; I cannot hear that!" cried Mr. Escott. "If it is so, Aura, your home is with your old father, and his arms and his heart shall shield you: to the last hour of my life, my own girl!—my poor Aura!—my poor child!"

"Dearest papa!" cried Aura, flinging her arms round his neck and burying her face against his shoulder; and then the desperate strength gave way, and she burst into tears in his arms.

"Don't cry, Aura love!" said Mrs. Escott kindly, patting her on the back as one does with children who choke. "I am sure nothing can be handsomer than your father's offer, and I am glad to see you feel it in that light; and I will help you with the children all I can; and of course they must be called Escotts then, and you Mrs. Aura Escott, I suppose; and no one can blame you, you know, when you didn't know anything about it."

But the Rector said gently; "Let her be, mother! let her be! God alone can comfort her."

"I know that, papa, without your telling me," snapped Mrs. Escott, affronted.

But though Aura was softened by her father's tenderness she was not swayed; and the two old people left the house no nearer their object than when they entered. She firmly refused to leave Croft (she would not even leave the grounds save for church on Sunday, she said) or to regard herself as other than Jasper Trelawney's lawful wife, unless proved beyond denial to be the contrary; which was not a pleasant state of things for them, considering their position in the parish, but, as matters stood, unavoidable. However, they determined on one thing in concert—to write to Herbert by the next mail, and beg him to come home and help them. They felt the thing was beyond them, and went into depths which they had no means of fathoming.

CHAPTER XI.

Mr. Grainger was uncomfortable. There was something in this strange arrival of Mr. Trelawney's so-called wife that roused up unpleasant feelings. It does not matter whether one can count the links or no, but the association of ideas influences us all, justly or unjustly; and the coming of the little Frenchwoman into this remote place in the same cycle as Mr. Dysart, and during his absence, troubled him. Not that he saw any reason to connect the two things together; but there was a certain indefinite relation between them in his own mind, though how formed, or on what based, he could not exactly tell. His whole energies were bent now on seeing this Madame de Chantreau, and talking

to her himself, trusting no other person's per-
spicacity or eyesight; but it was in vain that he
sought her.   He could not find her in field, lane,
or village, though he prowled about incessantly
like the ghost of an unburied peripatetic; and
people said : " Whatever was old Grainger after,
that he was in and out the town like a dog in
a fair—here, there, and everywhere ? "   All
Thursday, Friday, and Saturday forenoon he was
losing his time in looking for her; but Mr.
Bennet was spending many hours of each day
in her society, and Mrs. Price had called upon
her.

At last one Saturday afternoon as he was going
home to tea—the Vale dined early, save at the
Rectory and Croft; two o'clock being the usual
dinner hour of the smaller gentry—he saw a trim
little figure tripping on the road before him. At a
glance he knew that this must be the strange lady ;
she walked differently to the Vale ladies, with a
quicker, shorter, lighter step, something between
a running and a dancing step ; she wore her
shawl differently, and lifted her dress differently,

holding it in one hand over her left hip in the true French style, showing a petticoat that our grandmothers would have thought too airily handsome for anything but a ball dress, and a pair of the daintiest little feet in bronze kid boots, that ever inspired a shoemaker with enthusiasm and got their possessor unlimited credit. It was Madame Louise Trébuchet sure enough, on her way in the bright twilight to the Hollies, where she had been invited to a quiet tea as the best thing to be done for her at the present moment. Mrs. Price had thrown her whole soul into this matter, and was determined, she said, that Mr. Trelawney's true wife should lose nothing for want of countenance; knowing that under all the circumstances of the case, hers was the most influential countenance to be given her. It was certainly a bit of Nemesis that Mrs. Price of the Hollies should have constituted herself the protectress and social godmother of Louise Field, dite Trébuchet, Voleuse.

"Fine day, ma'am!" said Mr. Grainger overtaking her.

"Il fait très beau ce soir, monsieur," replied the clear, foreign voice; and Madame Louise turned her face sweetly towards him.

Mr. Grainger's sight grew a little dim, and his head swam round. How the deuce was it that she was so suggestive of his friend Dysart? It was not that she was like, but that she was suggestive. Was this then the secret that he had so often hinted at? Was this Madame de Chantreau—(queer name, very like cockcrow he thought to himself)—was she his relative? sister, cousin, niece, or what not? Oh, no!—that was impossible! Mr. Dysart was a gentleman, and she—had he not predetermined to find her an adventuress?—and had he ever failed in his judgments? Were not the Baron von Klugaugen, and now this Mr. Trelawney or Carthew or whatever the man's name was, guarantees of his insight? So Mr. Grainger put the suggestiveness behind him as a delusion of his own senses,— all people who had lived much abroad got a certain family likeness, being his self-reassurance, —and began with what was meant to be his artful drawing out.   Poor daft, conceit-blinded body!

"You have not been long at Clive Vale, ma'am, I think," he began.

"Non, monsieur, pas long-temps," said Madame Louise.

"And you like it, I hear?—and have found friends here?"

"It seems to me like home," replied Madame Louise, with a very strong foreign accent.

"An old friend of our neighbour Mr. Trelawney, hey?" continued Mr. Grainger in prosecution of his plan of drawing out.

She cast down her eyes modestly—"I am," she said.

"But you do not know Mrs. Trelawney?"

She looked up with her eyes wide open now; and what eyes they were!—how brilliant! how large! how expressive! but how sharp!

"Non, monsieur!" she answered coldly.

"Ah! she is worth seeing, ma'am," maliciously; "the handsomest young lady for miles round—looks like a goddess, and walks like a queen."

Madame's face grew dark, and her brilliant brown eyes squinted.

"I hear she is beautiful, poor lady," she said very icily.

"Beautiful! you may say that," exclaimed Mr. Grainger, scarcely understanding why, but delighted to tease and vex the Frenchwoman;—"tall, fair, stately,"—all in short that Madame Louise was not, implied.

The little woman looked annoyed and turned away her head. Mr. Patrick Grainger would have been rather discomfited if she had translated into the vernacular the thousand and one strange oaths she was pouring out against him in her own mind in French; and he would have scarcely recognised himself as a pig, and a block, and a grocer, and a polichinelle, and a hundred more—some of them not quite translateable.

"Mr. Dysart says she is the handsomest woman he has seen for years," said the tormentor, impelled by a strange impulse to use that gentleman's name suddenly, and mark its effect.

"Hein?" said Madame Louise.

"Mr. Dysart; don't you know Mr. Dysart, ma'am, and you an old friend of Mr. Trelawney's?" with a suspicious look and accent.

"Connais pas—I know him not," returned Madame Louise indifferently.

Mr. Grainger glanced at her sharply. Either she was telling a falsehood, he said to himself, or she had not been Mr. Trelawney's wife in his Paris days, when Mr. Dysart knew him and the children. Either way Mr. Grainger saw material for doubt and the foundation for future detection; and he looked as he felt, both suspicious and prophetically triumphant.

Madame Louise understood it all like a book. She had followed her brother's instructions in ignoring him, but she had imperilled her position with ce vieux bonhomme all the same; and he was evidently a partisan on the opposite side whom it would be gain to her to secure. From Gregory's account she had made sure of him— for of course she knew who he was; but she saw now that she had reckoned without her host, and charged nothing for the champagne.

"Monsieur qui? Monsieur Désar?" then said the little woman after a moment's rapid reflection, pronouncing the name in the French fashion. "A small dark gentleman, très coquet—what you English call a dandy, hey?"

"Yes, that will do for him," answered Mr. Grainger with a faint smile, not unwilling that even his friend Dysart should be quietly "taken down a peg," though he himself had made and polished and stuck into the social temple all the higher pegs on which his reputation hung, and though his taker-down was the woman whose enemy he had consecrated himself to be, reason or none. "Well then, you do know him after all, it seems?"

"I do not know him personellement, monsieur: but he was a friend of my hus—— of Monsieur Carthew—I should say—in former years I believe. I did not know at the first who you would indicate, but now I understand."

"A man of high position, I suppose?"

"Certainly," replied Madame Louise.

" Intimate with the Emperor, and all the ministers ? "

" Pas de doute," carelessly. " Monsieur Désar bears a name well known in Paris. Monsieur knows him then ?" lifting her eyes with the most bewitching simplicity of expression.

" He lives here," said Mr. Grainger; " and he and I are intimate friends."

" Vraiment ? "

" He is in London at present, but you must see him when he comes home," continued Mr. Grainger.

She smiled and bent her head; but the conversation about a man she knew nothing of did not particularly interest her, she implied; so the talk on the Emperor's private friend dropped as she wished that it should, not caring to have too much subject-matter for fencing on hand: Mr. Grainger winding up with what was meant to be anything but a comforting prospect—

"I will make a point of bringing Mr. Dysart to you when he returns, and then you can compare notes."

To which she replied;

"Merci, monsieur! I shall be very happy to see him," in a tone so tranquil, so careless, and assured, that Mr. Patrick was puzzled and all but thrown off the scent.

And then Madame Louise, being bored by his company and rather embarrassed by his enmity, wished him "good evening" in the blandest tones at her command, and turned down the lane leading to the Hollies, saying—

"They wait for me chez Madame Price. I hope that monsieur's pleasant company has not made me fail my visit," turning back with a laughing air that rather disconcerted Mr. Patrick.

On the whole then, this interview so much desired by Mr. Grainger had run off into sand, doing no good to any one. In the encounter of wits between himself and Madame Louise he was an infant where she was a veteran; and though she had not blinded him as her brother had done, and he was still as firmly as ever convinced that she was an impostor, that was owing to circumstances rather than to herself, and because she had fascinated Mr. Bennet to begin with. And it would be about as rational to expect water to run up hill, as Mr. Grainger and Mr. Bennet to pull together on any subject whatsoever. Thus, while the curate was becoming dangerously interested in the little woman, Patrick Grainger parted from her contemptuously, settled in his own mind as to her imposture and determined that she should be unmasked. But how?

When Madame Louise arrived at the Hollies to assist in that sacred institution of a "quiet tea," she found only Mr. Bennet and Major Morgan as her co-guests; not very lively companions, any of them, and but a poor promise of amusement for the evening. And yet it was good fun acting her part of the high-minded, noble-hearted woman, while laughing in her sleeve at them all for so many gobemouches ready to swallow the biggest flies, or ducks for the matter of that, to be turned out of the machine for lies; and it was good fun listening to all their insular prejudices against the French, about as true and just as prejudices usually are, especially when the people speaking know nothing

about the subject personally and only judge from
hearsay at any number of hands. She encouraged
them in their stupidities unmercifully, and played
their own game with consummate skill, rising
in respect with every stone cast at "those benighted
idolaters" as Mr. Bennet called them, and quite
agreeing that they were all untruthful and insin-
cere, unloving mothers, unfaithful wives, careless
husbands, undutiful children; that there was no
home-life among them, no order, cleanliness,
regularity, economy; that you could not believe
them, and you could not trust them; that they
were utterly irreligious, and that the priests and
the faith were about on a par; in fine, that she
lived there "for certain reasons she would rather
not enter into now," she said with a touching air—
implying either that she loved the scene of her
past happiness, or kept in view of her old friends,
or kept out of Mr. Trelawney's way, or any
other sublimity with which they chose to credit
her, but that her heart and habits and faith and
temper were all English—English to the back-
bone and deeper.

Poor Legrand of the Haymarket!—if he could have heard his vraie Parisienne blaspheming his great national altar to-night at the Hollies, he would have forsworn philanthropy for the future, and would have never trusted red-brown eyes again. There are some persons to whom lying and feigning is a luxury per se; and Madame Louise Trébuchet de Chantreau was one of them. But then she did it so well!

By the end of the evening she had achieved the success she had designed to achieve; and of the five persons forming that party—honest souls all of them, if mean and spiteful, and with the ordinary allowance of human intellect though narrowed and prejudiced—with them all this little Parisian thief and adventuress was taken as the representative of a cloud of womanly virtues, and as the victim of a cruel fraud. Only Miss Zillah and Miss Sara in their secret souls disliked her; which was quite natural, seeing where Mr. Bennet stood and which way Major Morgan was going. But their dislike meant envy, and envy is not distrust.

The next day was bright and brilliant, one of those glorious days of early autumn time when all things and all people gather abroad, as if there was an invisible fête somewhere to which they were bound to go. And because it was so bright and brilliant the church was crowded; all the farmers and cottagers from the outlying districts coming in for their three or four miles' walk, not grumbling at the distance to-day, which made the walk indeed all the pleasanter. It was sacrament Sunday too, and perhaps that helped; at all events the church was thronged, and every one in the place was there, save Mr. and Mrs. Escott. Mrs. Escott said she could not face the people; and the Rector felt that he could not take part in the service—he could not trust himself; so, not liking to go as merely one of the congregation leaving all the officiating to his curate, he absented himself as well as his wife; and both went over to the county town—they said on business; but the Vale knew better.

The church was full, and the knot of gossippers at the lych gate had wandered in one by one, but the service had not begun, when Mrs. Trelawney and her children entered. A kind of rustle and murmur went through the congregation as she walked up the aisle with her serene face and graceful bearing, holding Mabel by the hand, while Julia led Dotty, and Miss Tunstall followed. In general Aura herself took charge of the boy, as possessing the greater amount of authority over him, his nature being turbulent; and the people did not fail to mark the little difference, claiming as it did the unbroken unity of the family and her untouched rights over her step-children. It was not a pleasant ordeal for her as she walked up the church, all eyes bent on her and nudges and whispers following her; but she bore herself calmly and unflinchingly, thinking only of Jasper and how she must stand to her colours for his sake, and by the quietness of her manner discredit the assumption that she had any cause to fear or to fail.

So she went with her children; walking with the same step as usual, not slackened and not hastened; looking with the same calm eyes and untroubled brow, not defiantly, not boldly, but strong in the strength of love, and great in her dignity and innocence. And soon after she entered Mr. Bennet passed from the vestry to the reading desk and the service began.

The opening hymn was sung and the opening sentences were read, and Mr. Bennet had got about half way through the exhortation, when the rustle of silk was heard at the side-door, and a woman's light step came half uncertainly, as a stranger does come, into the church; and a pretty little dark face, veiled beneath a transparent veil, looked appealingly round, asking mutely for guidance and reception. The side-door, where this little figure stood, just faced Mr. Grainger's seat; and the great square red pew of Croft, was some three or four farther up the chancel. Julia sat next the pew door—Aura in the corner in a line with her; Mabel, Dotty, and Miss Tunstall were opposite. Aura had not looked up when the silk rustled and the feet pattered; she seldom looked about her at church, and perhaps to-day she did not care to see more than she was obliged; but

Julia's quick eyes saw it all :—the entrance, the mute appeal, and then the glad recognition as the foreign lady's eye met hers, and she smiled and gently bowed her head. Flushed and eager the child opened the pew door, and Madame Louise Trébuchet de Chantreau glided in. Then Aura looked up and saw who her guest was, standing. now facing the congregation in the space between Julia and herself—the three in a line together.

It was something like a deep drawn breath that went through the church, and even Mr. Bennet's voice trembled ; Aura for a moment crimsoned to her temples, but the next she was as white as the sculptured corbel on the wall before her. She never winced, though she knew all eyes were on her ; but her hands holding her prayer-book trembled, and she stood with less than her usual flexible grace and more than natural rigidity. Only when Julia offered Madame Louise half her prayer-book, and the lady tenderly smiling took her hand in hers and kept it, while with her looks caressing Mabel—only then a sharp pang carried the flush of failure over her for a moment; but she recovered herself from this too, and no one could read her more. So they stood through the service, the strangest and the saddest group the Vale had ever seen.

Little of abstracted devotion was there in that congregation to-day; the contrast in the Croft pew occupying all minds, and engaging all eyes. Of the two women standing there, which was rightful owner?—that pretty little dark creature with her brilliant eyes and her raven hair, so piquante, so foreign, so well dressed in the trim, tight-fitting, well-considered way of Frenchwomen —not a hair out of its place, not a bow too many, not an inharmonious colour, not a superfluous streamer anywhere, and yet all so rich and sufficing?—or Aura, tall, fair, stately, with the long curls of golden brown hair on her shoulders, her costume of violet and white looser in its fit and more pictorially beautiful than madame's but less professionally correct, so queenly, so Greek, so royal in her womanhood, with her face so full of love and dignity and depth, where her rival's was all sparkling with vivacity, and bright and clever but not deep?—which was the true wife? which the true mother?

For the last there was soon no doubt in the mind of any. For when Madame Louise threw up her veil, standing close by the side of Julia, the whole church could see for themselves that they were of the same type and race, tempered indeed by the greater largeness and power of the father, but substantively of the same family. Nature too said something in the strange way in which the children took to her; for though taught to be genial and gracious to all people, the girls were naturally distant and haughty, and had to be continually reminded of the grace of humility and the beauty of charity. There was no need to remind them in this instance. They were almost in madame's arms, and could scarcely take their eyes from her during the service; and more than one mother in the congregation felt her eyelids wet as she pictured what *this* mother must feel so near to her children, and yet so separated!

Just before the sermon began, while the last hymn was being sung and Mr. Bennet was changing the surplice for the gown, the sexton, who officiated as verger and rober, brought Aura a small pencilled scrap of paper—a bit of the sermon-sheet hastily torn off and addressed to her in Mr. Bennet's handwriting.

Mabel handed it to her, and she opened it naturally enough ; to read these words nervously and hurriedly scrawled :

" DEAR MADAM,

" UNDER the painful circumstances of your present position, the danger and sin of which it is evident you do not, and will not, recognize, I must, as a conscientious minister of God, refuse to administer the Holy Sacrament to you to-day. Spare me therefore the pain of a public rejection, and yourself the humiliation, and do not remain among the devout and penitent confessors of their sins.

" Yours very truly,

" Z. S. BENNET."

His name was Zachariah Simeon.

But Louise Field, Voleuse, did stay; and Mr. Bennet blessed her with a special blessing as she knelt against the altar rails, quiet, devout, and tearful.

END OF VOL. II.

London: Printed by SMITH, ELDER AND Co., Old Bailey, E C.